The Ghost of Grania O'Malley

MICHAEL MORPURGO

EGMONT

To Alice and Lucie –
welcome to the world

As she says herself, there are many spellings of Grania
O'Malley's name. The spelling used in this book is an English
Translation of her name from the Irish Language.

EGMONT
We bring stories to life

First published in Great Britain in 1996 by Macmillan Eductaion Ltd
This edition published 2007 by Egmont UK Limited
239 Kensington High Street, London W8 6SA

Text Copyright © 1996 Michael Morpurgo
Cover illustration copyright © 2007 Lee Gibbons

The moral rights of the author and cover illustrator have been asserted

ISBN 978 1 4052 3340 8

5 7 9 10 8 6 4

www.egmont.co.uk
www.michaelmorpurgo.org

A CIP catalogue record for this title is available from the British Library

Printed and bound in Great Britain by the CPI Group

EGMONT PRESS: ETHICAL PUBLISHING

Egmont Press is about turning writers into successful authors and children into passionate readers – producing books that enrich and entertain. As a responsible children's publisher, we go even further, considering the world in which our consumers are growing up.

Safety First
Naturally, all of our books meet legal safety requirements. But we go further than this; every book with play value is tested to the highest standards – if it fails, it's back to the drawing-board.

Made Fairly
We are working to ensure that the workers involved in our supply chain – the people that make our books – are treated with fairness and respect.

Responsible Forestry
We are committed to ensuring all our papers come from environmentally and socially responsible forest sources.

For more information, please visit our website at www.egmont.co.uk/ethical

Mixed Sources
Product group from well-managed forests and other controlled sources
www.fsc.org Cert no. TT-COC-002332
© 1996 Forest Stewardship Council

Egmont is passionate about helping to preserve the world's remaining ancient forests. We only use paper from legal and sustainable forest sources, so we know where every single tree comes from that goes into every paper that makes up every book.

This book is made from paper certified by the Forestry Stewardship Council (FSC), an organisation dedicated to promoting responsible management of forest resources. For more information on the FSC, please visit **www.fsc.org**. To learn more about Egmont's sustainable paper policy, please visit **www.egmont.co.uk/ethical**.

CONTENTS

1 SMILEY

JESSIE WAS ALWAYS FINDING BONES IN THE
great bog-oak field where they dug the peat for the winter
fires. It was here too that her father found most of the
wood he needed for his wood sculptures, his 'creatures' as
she called them. She was forever going off there alone,
mooching around, bottom in the air looking for her
bones. She had a whole collection of them, but she never
tired of looking for more. Mostly they were just sheep
bones – skulls, jawbones, legbones, vertebrae. She had
shrews' skulls too, birds' skulls, all sorts of skulls. But
there was one skull she found that was unlike any other,
because it was a human skull. She was quite sure of it.

She never said a word to anyone. She kept it with the

rest of her collection in the ruined cottage at the bottom of the bog-oak field. No one but herself ever went near the place. She called him Smiley because he would keep grinning at her. She put Smiley in pride of place in a niche in the cottage wall; and from time to time she'd go and talk to him and tell him her troubles – which were many. Smiley would listen, stare back at her and say nothing, which was what she wanted.

But as time passed, Jessie began to feel more and more uneasy about Smiley. So one day, in confession, she told Father Gerald about her skull, partly because she'd been worrying herself about it, and partly because at the time she could think of no other sins to confess. If she told him she had done nothing wrong, nothing bad enough to confess, he just wouldn't believe her. She'd tried that before. So she blurted it out about Smiley, told him everything; but she could tell from the tone of his voice that he just thought this was another of Jessie Parsons' little white lies.

'Bones should be buried in hallowed ground and left undisturbed, Jessie,' he said sonorously. 'Then the souls of the departed can rest in peace.'

So, one dark night with the owl hooting at her from high up in the ruined abbey, she dug a small hole under the abbey walls, said goodbye to Smiley in a whisper, laid him carefully in the wet earth and covered him up. She felt a lot better afterwards; and although she did miss him for a while, she felt pleased with herself that she'd done the right thing.

Some time later Father Gerald had asked after the skull and she'd shown him one of her many sheep's skulls. He'd laughed. 'It's as I thought, Jessie Parsons, that's never a human being. Do you not know a sheep's skull when you see one?' He'd counted the teeth carefully. 'I'd say that's a six-year-old ewe, by the teeth in her.'

Jessie went and put flowers on the unmarked grave just once. 'I hope you're feeling better now, Smiley,' she said. 'I'll leave you be, so's you can rest in peace, like Father Gerald says.' So she did, and as the weeks and months passed, she thought of Smiley less and less.

All this happened a year or more before the rest of it began.

2 THE BIG HILL

THERE HAD TO BE MIST OR JESSIE WOULD NOT even try it. If she failed, and so far she had always failed, she wanted no one else to know of it, especially her mother and father. She'd lost count of how many times she'd lied to them about the Big Hill, about how she had made it all the way to the top. They mustn't see her. No one must see her. If she was going to fail again, then she would fail alone and unseen.

Old Mister Barney might see her, and probably often did, as she passed his shack at the bottom of the Big Hill, but he'd be the only one; and besides, he wouldn't tell anyone. Mister Barney kept himself to himself and minded his own business. He hardly ever spoke to a soul.

Jessie was ten and he had spoken to her maybe half a dozen times in her entire life. He would wave at her through the window sometimes, but she was as sure as she could be that he would never spy on her. He just wasn't like that. There was smoke coming from his chimney and one of the chickens stood one-legged in the porch; but today, as Jessie walked across the clearing outside his shack, there was no sign of Mister Barney.

The mist cut the hill off halfway up and dwarfed it, but Jessie knew what was waiting for her up there, how high it really was, how hard it was going to be, and was daunted by it all over again. Mole, her mother's black donkey, nudged her from behind. Mole would go with her. He went everywhere with her. More than once it had been Mole who had spoilt it, nudging her off balance at just the wrong moment.

There was a lot that annoyed her about her 'lousy palsy', as she often called it. But it was balance that was the real problem. Once she'd fallen over, it took so much of her energy to get up again that there was little left for the Big Hill itself. If she could just keep her rhythm going – one and two, one and two, one and two – if she could just keep on lurching, and not fall over, she knew that one day, some day, she'd have strength enough to reach the top of the Big Hill, and then she'd never have to lie about it again.

Mole rubbed his nose up against her back. 'All right, Mole,' said Jessie, clutching the donkey's neck to steady herself. 'I'm going. I'm going. It's all very well for you. You've got four good legs. I've only got two, and they won't exactly do what I tell them, will they?' She looked up at the Big Hill and took a deep breath. 'I'm telling you, Mole, today's the day. I can feel it inside me.' The donkey glanced at her and snorted. Jessie laughed. 'Race you to the top, big ears.'

She started well enough, leaning forward into the hill, willing her fumbling feet forward. She knew every rut and tussock of the track ahead – she'd sat down hard enough on most of them. Mole walked alongside her, browsing in the bracken. After a while he trotted on ahead, all tippy-toed, and disappeared into the mist. 'Clever clogs!' Jessie called after him, but then she tried all she could to put him out of her mind. She knew she had to concentrate. The path was wet from the mist, and slippery. One false step and she'd be on her bottom and that would be that – again.

She could hear Mole snorting somewhere up ahead. As like as not, he'd be at the waterfall by now. Jessie had reached the waterfall just once, the week before – it was as high as she'd ever gone on her own. That time, too, her legs had let her down. They wouldn't manage the stones and she'd tripped and fallen. She'd tried crawling, but she wasn't any better at crawling than she was at walking. She'd crawled on through the water, become too cold and had had to give up. Today would be different. Today she would not let herself give up. Today she would reach the top, no matter what. Today she would prove to Mrs Burke, to Marion Murphy, and to everyone else at school that she could climb the Big Hill just like they could.

She could see Mole up ahead of her now, drinking in the pool below the waterfall. Jessie's legs ached. She wanted so much to stop, but she knew that she mustn't, that rhythm was everything. She passed Mole and laughed out loud at him. 'Haven't you read the one about the hare and the tortoise?' she cried. 'See you at the top.' This was the spot where she'd come to grief the week before, the part of the track she most dreaded. The track rose steeply beside the waterfall, curling away out of sight and around the back of the hill. Every stone was loose here and until she reached the waterfall, *if* she reached the waterfall, the track would be more like a stream, the stones under her feet more like stepping stones. From now on she would have to be careful, very careful.

She was standing now on the very rock where she'd tripped last time. She punched the air with triumph and staggered on, on and up. She was in unknown territory now. Only on her father's back had she ever gone beyond this point and that was a long time ago when she was small. She felt her legs weakening all the while. She fought them, forcing them on. She breathed in deep, drawing what strength she could from the air, and that was when the mist filled her lungs. She coughed and had to go on coughing. Still she tried to go on.

She felt herself falling and knew she could do nothing about it. She threw her arm out to save herself and was relieved to see she was falling into the water. She would be wet, but at least she wasn't going to hurt herself. But she hadn't accounted for the stone just beneath the surface of the water. She never even felt the cold of the stream as it covered her face. There was an explosion of pain inside her head and a ringing in her ears that seemed as if it would never end. Then the world darkened suddenly around her. She tried to see through it, but she couldn't. She tried to breathe, but she couldn't.

She was dreaming of her father's 'creature' sculptures. They were all in the cottage and Smiley was telling them a story and they were laughing, cackling like witches. She woke suddenly. She was sitting propped up, her back against a boulder. Mole was grazing some way off, his tail whisking. Jessie's head throbbed and she put her hand to it. There was a lump under her fingers, and it was sticky with blood. There was more blood in her ear and on her cheek too. She was soaked to the skin. She wondered for some moments where she was and how she had got there. She remembered the climb up the Big Hill, and how she had fallen; and she realised then that she had failed yet again. Tears filled her eyes and she cried out loud, her fists clenched, her eyes closed to stop the tears.

She tasted the salt of her tears and brushed them away angrily. 'I'll get there, Mrs Burke,' she shouted. 'I'll get there, you'll see.'

From nowhere came a voice, a woman's voice, but almost low enough to be a man's. 'Course you will, Jessie,' it said. 'But not if you sit there feeling all sorry for yourself.' Jessie looked around her. There was no one there. Mole glanced at her quizzically. He had stopped chomping. For one silly moment, Jessie imagined it might have been Mole talking, but then the voice went on. 'So you've a bit of a knock on your head. Are you going to let that stop you?' Mole was browsing again, tearing at the grass. So it couldn't be him talking. 'I'm not the donkey, Jessie. And I'll tell you something else for nothing, there's no point at all in your looking for me. You'll not find me. I'm just a voice, that's all. Don't go worrying about it.'

'Who are you?' Jessie whispered, sitting up and wiping her nose with the back of her hand.

'Is that what they teach children these days? Can you not use a handkerchief like a proper person? Have you not got a handkerchief?'

'Yes,' said Jessie, still looking all around her, but frantically now.

'Then use it, why don't you?' Jessie searched out her handkerchief and blew her nose. 'That's better now,' the voice went on. 'I've always thought that you can tell a lot about folk from the way they treat their noses. There's pickers, there's wipers – like you – there's snifflers and, worst of all, there's trumpeters. You'll not believe this, but I once knew a queen, a real queen, I'm telling you – and she was a trumpeter. Worse still, she'd blow her nose on a handkerchief and she wouldn't throw it away like you or me. She'd use it again, honest she would. She'd use the same handkerchief twice. Can you believe such a thing? And herself a queen! I told her straight out. I said: "There's no surer way to catch a cold and die than to use the same handkerchief twice." She was no one's fool, that queen. Oh no, she listened to me. She must have, because she lived on and into a ripe old age, just like me. She died sitting up. Did you know that?'

Chuckling now, the voice seemed to be coming closer all the time. 'That queen, she wouldn't lie down for anyone, not even death. A lady after my own heart she was. English, mind, but she couldn't help that now, could she? Listen, Jessie, are you just going to sit there or are you going to get up on your feet and climb the Big Hill, like you said you would?'

'Who are you?' Jessie asked again. She was hoping against hope that maybe she was still asleep and dreaming it all. But she *was* bleeding and there *was* real blood on her fingers, on her head. So the voice had to be real too – unless she was going mad. That thought, that she might be going mad, frightened Jessie above everything else.

'It doesn't matter who I am,' said the voice, and it came from right beside her now, 'except that this is my hill you're walking on. I've been watching you these last weeks, we all have, the boys and me. They didn't think you'd make it, but I did. I was sure of it, so sure of it that I've a wager on it – five gold doubloons. And, Jessie, if there's one thing I hate losing, it's money. And here you are, sitting there like a pudding, crying your eyes out and wiping your nose with the back of your hand. I'm ashamed of you, Jessie.'

'I'm sorry,' said Jessie. 'I didn't mean to . . .'

'So you should be. I tell you what.' The voice was whispering in her ear. 'I'll make it worth your while. I'll leave a little something for you at the top of the hill. But if you want my little something, then you'll have to go up there and fetch it for yourself. How about it?'

Jessie was still thinking about what she should do when she felt strong arms under her shoulders, lifting her on to her feet and then holding her for a moment until she had steadied herself on her legs. Then someone tapped her bottom. 'On your way, girl.' And Jessie found herself walking on, almost without meaning to, as if her legs were being worked by someone else. She looked behind her again and again to see if anyone was there. There was no one, only Mole ambling along, head lowered, ears back.

'Did you hear her?' Jessie whispered, as Mole came alongside. 'She's watching us, I know she is. Come on Mole, we've *got* to get to the top, we've got to.' And she lurched on up the Big Hill, rejoining the track beyond the waterfall.

The grass under her feet was spongy here; easier walking, easier falling too, she thought. She remembered how her father had galloped her on his back along this same grassy path, and how they'd fallen over and rolled down the hill together and into the bracken. She remembered too the rockstrewn gully ahead, and wondered how she was ever going to get past it. She went down on her hands and knees. It would be painful and slow, but it was the only way. There were brambles across the path that had to be pulled away, endless lacerating rocks to be negotiated. Jessie kept crawling until her wrists couldn't take it any more and she had to crawl on her elbows. That was when her knee slipped and her fingers wouldn't grasp and she slid backwards. She ended up in an ungainly heap, wedged against the rocks, knees and elbows barked and bleeding, and a vicious thorn stuck in the palm of her hand. She drew it out with her teeth and spat it on to the ground.

Mole was braying at her from somewhere further up the hill. Jessie looked up, shielding her eyes against the white of the sun that was breaking now through the mist. Mole was standing right on top of the Big Hill. He wasn't just calling her, he was taunting her. Jessie levered herself laboriously to her feet and swayed there for a moment, her head spinning. She closed her eyes, and then it all came flooding back.

April, the start of the summer term at school and they'd all of them gone, even the infants, up the Big Hill on a nature walk with Mrs Burke, her head teacher and the other bane of her life besides Marion Murphy. And Jessie had been the only one to be left behind with Miss Jefferson, the infant teacher. Miss Jefferson had insisted on holding her hand all the way to the beach, just in case, she said. They were going to find lots of interesting shells, she said, to make a shell picture. It was always shells or wild flowers with Miss Jefferson – she had her own wild flower meadow behind the school. But today it was shells.

Miss Jefferson foraged through the bladderwrack and the sea lettuce, whooping with joy every few seconds and talking nineteen to the dozen like she always did. It wasn't that Jessie didn't like her; she did. But she was forever fussing her, endlessly anxious that Jessie might fall, might be too cold, might be too tired. Jessie was used to that, used to her. It was being left behind that she really resented.

Despite all Miss Jefferson's enthusiastic encouragement she could not bring herself to care a fig about the shell picture. She wanted to be up there with them, with the others. All the while she kept her eye on the Big Hill. She could see them, a trail of children up near the summit now, Mrs Burke striding on ahead. She heard the distant cheer when they reached the top and she had to look away. Miss Jefferson understood and put her arm round her, but it was no comfort.

She had begged to be allowed to go up the Big Hill with the others, but Mrs Burke wouldn't even hear of it. 'You'd slow us down, Jessie,' she'd said. 'And besides, you know you'd never reach the top.' And then she'd laughed. 'And I'm afraid you're far too big to carry.' That was the moment Jessie had decided she would climb the Big Hill, cerebral lousy palsy or not. Somehow or other she would do it, she'd drag herself up there if necessary.

She opened her eyes. Here she was, after two months of trying, within a stone's throw of the summit. This time there'd be no stopping her. 'Here I come!' she cried. 'Here I come!' And she launched herself up the hill. Several times her legs refused to do what she told them and threatened to buckle beneath her. Time and again, she felt herself reeling. She longed just to sit down and rest; but again and again she heard the voice in her head. 'You can do it, girl, you can do it.'

Where the words came from, or who spoke them, she neither knew nor cared any more. Nothing mattered but getting to the top. She was almost there when her legs simply folded on her, and she found herself on her knees. She crawled the last metre or so over mounds of soft thrift and then collapsed. Mole came over to her and nuzzled her neck with his warm whiskery nose. She clung to Mole's mane and hauled herself up on to her feet.

There below her lay the whole of Clare Island, and all around the grey-green sea, with the island of Inishturk far to the south. And when she turned her face into the wind, there was the mainland and the islands of Clew Bay floating in the sea like distant dumplings. She was on top of the world. She lifted her hands to the sky and laughed out loud and into the wind, the tears running down her face. Mole looked on, each of his ears turning independently. Jessie's legs collapsed and she sat down with a sudden jolt that knocked the breath out of her for a moment, and stunned her into sanity.

Only then did she begin to reflect on all that had happened to her on the Big Hill that morning. There could be no doubt that she had made it to the top, unless of course she was still in the middle of some wonderful dream. But the more she thought about it, the more she began to doubt her memory of the climb, the fall in the stream, the disembodied voice that had spoken to her, the arms that had helped her to her feet, the words in her head that had urged her on to the top. It could all have been some extraordinary hallucination. That would make sense of it. But then, what about the bump on her head? And there was something else she couldn't understand. Someone must have rescued her from the stream. But who? Maybe it was all the bump on the head, maybe that was why she was hearing voices. And maybe that was why her memory was deceiving her. She had to be sure, really sure. She had to test it.

'Hello?' she ventured softly. 'Are you still there? I did it, didn't I? I won your bet for you. Are you there?' There was no one, nothing, except a solitary humming bumble-bee, a pair of gulls wheeling overhead and Mole munching nearby. Jessie went on, 'Are you anyone? Are you someone? Are you just a bump on the head or what? Are you real? Say something, please.' But no one said anything. Something rustled behind her. Jessie swung round and saw a rabbit scuttling away into the bracken, white tail bobbing. She noticed there were rabbit droppings all over the summit. She flicked at one of them and it bounced off the side of a rock, a giant granite rock shaped by the wind and weather into a perfect bowl, and in the bowl was a pool of shining water fed by a spring from above it.

Jessie hadn't been thirsty until now. She crawled over, grasped the lip of the rock and hauled herself up. She put her mouth into the water like Mole did and drank deep. Water had never been so welcome to her as it was that morning on the summit of the Big Hill. She was wiping her mouth when she saw something glinting at the bottom of the pool. It looked like a large ring, brass maybe, like one of the curtain rings they had at home in the sitting room. She reached down into the water and picked it out.

'I am a woman of my word.' The same voice, from behind her somewhere. 'Didn't I say I'd leave a little something for you?' In her exhaustion, in her triumph,

Jessie had quite forgotten all about the promised 'little something'. She backed herself up against the rock. 'Don't be alarmed, Jessie, I'll not hurt you. I've never hurt a single soul that didn't deserve it. You did a fine thing today, Jessie, a fine thing; and what's better still, you won me my wager. I'm five gold doubloons richer, not that I've a lot to spend it on, mind. None of us have, but that's by the by. None of the boys thought you could do it, but I did. And I like to be right. It's a family failing of ours. "Her mother's an O'Malley," I told them. "So Jessie's half an O'Malley. She'll do it, just watch." And we did watch and you did do it. The earring's yours, girl. To be honest with you I've not a lot of use for such things these days. Look after it, won't you?'

When Jessie spoke at last, her voice was more of a whisper than she had intended it to be. 'Where are you? Can't I see you? You can't be just a voice.' But there was no reply. She tried again and again, until she knew that whoever had been there either didn't want to answer or had gone away. 'Thanks for the earring,' Jessie called out. 'I won't lose it, I promise.'

It should have sounded silly talking to no one like she was, but somehow it didn't. Talking to Mole was silly and she knew it, but there was no one else and she had to talk to someone. 'See what she gave me, Mole? It's an earring.

It's because I climbed the Big Hill and she won her bet.'
The donkey lifted his upper lip, showed his yellow teeth
and sniffed suspiciously at the ring in the flat of Jessie's
hand. He decided it wasn't worth eating.

Jessie looked back down the Big Hill. It was a very
long way back down again. She had never given a single
thought as to how she would get down if ever she got to
the top, probably because in her heart of hearts she had
never really believed she *would* get to the top. She knew
well enough that, for her, climbing down the stairs at
home was always a more difficult proposition than
climbing up. She'd never manage it, not all the way to the
bottom. It was impossible. Then she had an idea, an
obvious idea, but a good one. Mole would take her down.
She would use the rock as a mounting block, lie over
Mole's back and hitch a ride all the way back home. Easy.

It did not prove as easy as she had imagined. First of
all, Mole wouldn't come to the rock and had to be
dragged there by his mane. Then he wouldn't stand still,
not at first. Mole wasn't at all used to being ridden and
shifted nervously under Jessie's weight; but eventually he
seemed to get the idea and walked away, taking Jessie
down the Big Hill and all the way back home, Jessie
clinging on like a limpet, desperate not to slide off. She
waited until Mole was grazing the grass on the lawn in

amongst her father's 'creatures', and then just dropped off. It was a fairly painless landing. That was where her father found her when he came back from the sheep field a short time later.

'Didn't you see me, Dad?' she said.

He stared at her in horror. 'There's blood all over you, Jess,' he said, running over to her. 'What have you been up to?'

'I did it, Dad. I climbed the Big Hill! Mole brought me back, but I did the rest all on my own.'

'I thought you'd climbed it already,' said her father. In her excitement, Jessie had even forgotten her own lies.

'I did,' she said, recovering quickly, 'I did, but I did it again, faster this time.'

Her father carried her inside and sat her down in the kitchen. 'What do you want to go and do a crazy thing like that for?' he said, dabbing her grazed knees with wet cotton wool. It should have stung, but it didn't. 'Your mother will kill me, letting you go off like that. Don't you say a word about it when she gets back, you hear me? And just look at the lump on your head!'

Jessie clutched the earring tight in her fist. The sheepdog was sniffing at it. 'Get off, Panda,' she said, pushing him away. Panda gazed up at her out of his two white eyes and rested his wet chin on her knee. He'd been rolling in something nasty again. 'When's Mum back?' Jessie went on.

'This evening, if the weather holds,' said her father, pressing a cool tea towel on her head. 'Here, hold that. It'll get the swelling down. He's arrived. Your cousin, Jack. Your mum rang from the airport at Shannon.'

'What's he like?' Jessie said. Panda was trying to lick his way into her fist. She pushed him away again.

'Quiet, doesn't say very much. Make a change from you, won't it?'

'All summer!' Jessie protested. 'Why does he have to come all summer?'

'Because he's a relation, your Uncle Sean's son, your cousin.'

'But I've never even met Uncle Sean.' Her father lifted up her arm to examine her elbow. She pulled away. 'I'll wash it myself,' she snapped.

'What's the matter, Jess?' he asked, crouching down beside her.

'I wish he didn't have to come, Dad,' she said. 'I like it like it is, with just the three of us.'

'Me too,' said her father. 'But we'll be three again after he's gone, won't we? Now get upstairs and wash that elbow of yours. We don't want it going poisonous on us. Your mum'll have fifty fits.'

Jessie had already thought where she would hide the earring before she even reached her room. The goldfish bowl. She'd hide it in the stones at the bottom of Barry's bowl. Barry went mad while she was doing it. He always hated her putting her hand in his bowl. 'Look after it for me, Barry,' she said, and the goldfish mouthed at her from under his wispy weed and then turned his tail on her. 'Please yourself then,' she said. All the while, Panda was on her bed and watching her intently. 'Secret,' she said, putting her finger to her lips. 'No one must ever know, just you and me and Barry. He's not telling anyone and neither are you, are you? You stink, Panda, you know that?'

3 THE FACE IN THE MIRROR

CLATTERBANG WOULDN'T START. SHE NEVER did when there was mist about, and there was often mist about. Clatterbang was a rusty old black taxicab that had seen better days on the streets of London and Belfast, but she was perfect for the island – when she worked. You could carry up to six sheep in the back, or twelve bales of hay, or a 'creature' sculpture. But today it was just Jessie, with Panda curled up beside her on the back seat. Her father had his head under the bonnet, and said something that he would never have dared say if her mother had been home. He tried whatever he was trying again and suddenly the engine started. He slammed the bonnet down and jumped in.

'We'll be late,' he said. 'Hold tight.' They bumped and rattled down the farm track, out on to the road, past the abbey ruins and along the coast road towards the quay. They weren't late. The ferry was just tying up. Her father stopped the car and turned to her. 'Once more, Jess, how'd you get the bump?'

'I fell over.'

'Where?'

'In the garden.'

'Good. And you stick to that story, no matter what, understand?'

They could see her mother now, tying her scarf over her head. She was standing at the end of the quay, and beside her was a tall boy, almost as tall as she was, with a white baseball hat on, sideways. He was gazing around him, hands thrust deep into his pockets. 'Will you look at that beanpole of a boy!' said Jessie's father, opening the car door. 'I'll give her a hand with those bags. You wait here.' And he was gone.

Jessie got out of the car and tottered along after him as fast as she could, which wasn't fast at all. Her legs were still tired from the climb up the Big Hill. She glanced up at the Big Hill, but it was no longer there. The mist had cut off its top again. She thought then of the voice and heard it again in her head. The more she thought about it, the more she believed it must be the first sign of madness. Maybe she had cerebal palsy of the brain as well as the body. Or maybe it was the voice of a saint she had heard. She hoped it was that. She'd heard the stories of St Patrick talking to folk as they climbed up Crough Patrick just over the water on the mainland. If it could happen there, it could happen here. It wasn't impossible. But then she thought that the voice hadn't sounded at all like a saint, not Jessie's idea of a saint anyway.

They were all three coming towards her now, her father carrying the bags, her mother striding out ahead, almost running as she reached her. 'What do you mean, she fell over?' she said. Then she was crouching down in front of her and holding her by the shoulders. 'Are you all right, Jess?'

'Fine, Mum.'

'What happened?'

'I just tripped, that's all.'

'Where?'

'In the garden.' Jessie didn't dare look up in case she caught her father's eye. Her mother was examining the lump on her head. 'One week,' she went on, 'I go away one week. Have you seen the doctor?'

'No.'

'Dizzy?'

'No.'

Then the boy was standing there. He had a silver brace on his teeth – more brace than teeth, Jessie thought.

'This is your cousin Jack,' said her mother, smiling now. 'All the way from Long Island, New York, America, to Clare Island, County Mayo, Ireland, isn't that right, Jack?' The boy was staring at her, and frowning at the same time. It was a normal reaction, when people saw her first. It was the way she stood, a little lopsided, as if she was disjointed somehow.

'Hi,' said the boy. He was still scrutinising her. 'How are you?'

'Fine,' said Jessie. 'Why wouldn't I be?'

'She's not fine at all,' said her mother, and she smoothed Jessie's hair out of her face. 'She's a terrible lump on her head.' Panda jumped up at Jack, and the boy backed away in alarm.

'He won't hurt you,' said Jessie. 'Only a sheepdog, not a wolf, y'know.' Jack laughed, a little nervously, Jessie thought.

'We've got bigger ones back home,' he said, recovering himself. 'We've got wolfhounds, Irish wolfhounds, three of them.'

'Well, one's good enough for us,' Jessie said. 'He's called Panda.'

'On account of his eyes, I guess,' said Jack.

'Not necessarily,' said Jessie, unwilling to hide her irritation.

'We'll be home in a few minutes, Jack,' said Jessie's father. 'Nowhere's far on Clare Island. Four miles end to end.' He put the bags down, and flexed his fingers. 'You can walk the whole island in a couple of hours. I've got Clatterbang down the end of the quay, by the castle there.'

Jessie felt the boy watching her walk. She looked up quickly to catch him at it. She was right. He *was* watching. 'You play American football?' she asked. It was just something to say.

'Some.'

'I've seen it on the telly. You any good at it?'

'Not that good.'

'Makes two of us then, doesn't it?' she said. She smiled at him and got a ghost of a smile back. Perhaps she liked him a little better now than she had at first, but she still wasn't sure of him. She eyed him warily as he walked along beside her in his spongy trainers, shoulders hunched. His hair was cut close. It was so close and so fair she could see every contour of his head, and he had more freckles on him than Jessie had ever seen on anyone. He was thin too, so that his blue jeans and his New York Yankees pinstripe sweatshirt hung loose on him. He was pointing up at the castle now. 'Who lives up there?' he said. 'Looks kind of old.'

'It is. No one lives there, not any more.'

Jessie's father had stopped by the car and was opening the door. 'Jeez, that's some car,' Jack said, running his hand along the bonnet. 'Diesel, right? Three-litre engine? Old, I guess.'

'It goes,' Jessie snapped. 'And that's all a car's got to do, isn't it?' Now she had quite definitely made up her mind. She did not like this boy. She would not like this boy, she wouldn't ever like this boy. This was going to be the longest month of her life. Her mother was giving her one of her pointed looks.

'You two cousins getting on, are you?' she said.

'Perfect,' said Jessie, and she got in the car and slammed the door, leaving Jack to walk round the other side.

Clatterbang spluttered a few times and then started up reluctantly. No one spoke until they were well along the coast road.

'Miss me?' said Jessie's mother.

'Missed you,' her father replied. 'We both did, didn't we, Jess?' He turned to her. 'And how was Dublin?'

'Don't ask.' She spoke so quietly that Jessie could hardly hear.

On the back seat, cousin Jack and cousin Jessie sat side by side in silence. Panda looked first at one and then the other. At supper, Jack hardly touched a thing. He chewed on a piece of bread and said it wasn't the same as the bread 'back home'. The water, he said, tasted 'kind of funny' and he screwed up his nose when Jessie's father offered him some of his home-made sheep's cheese.

'You got peanut butter?' Jack asked. 'I usually have peanut butter sandwiches and a Coke.'

'What, every meal?' Jessie's father said.

Jack nodded. 'Except breakfast. I have cornflakes for breakfast, and Coke.'

'I'll get some peanut butter in tomorrow,' Jessie's mother said, patting his arm. 'Now you'd better get yourself to bed. A good night's sleep, that's what you need. Got to be up early. School tomorrow.'

'School?'

'That's what your father said,' Jessie's mother went on. '"Treat him no different," he told me. "What Jessie does, he does." Your dad's my older brother, remember? I always did what he said when I was little – almost always anyway – and where you're concerned, what your dad says goes. So it's school for you tomorrow. Jess will be with you. You'll look after him, won't you, Jess? You need any help unpacking, Jack?' Jack shook his head. Then, without saying a word, he stood up, pushed back his chair and went out. The three of them looked at each other, the clock ticking behind them in the silence of the kitchen. They heard Jack's bedroom door shut at the end of the passage upstairs.

'He's got his troubles,' Jessie's mother said. 'He'll be fine, he'll settle.'

'What kind of troubles?' Jessie asked.

'Never you mind,' and she tapped Jessie's plate. 'Waste not, want not. Eat. And by the way, Jess, will you tell me how come your trousers are all torn and covered in mud?'

'I told you. I fell over, I tripped,' Jessie said, suddenly busying herself with her eating so she didn't have to look up.

'In the garden,' her father added, rather too hurriedly.

'So you said, so you said.' It was quite clear she didn't believe a word of it.

Jessie's bedroom was right above the kitchen. She could always hear what was being said downstairs, even if sometimes she didn't want to. But tonight she did. She knew – everyone on the island knew – the real reason her mother had been over to the mainland. It wasn't just to fetch cousin Jack from the airport. That was just part of it.

She'd been a whole week in Dublin, trying to see the bigwigs in the Dáil, the parliament, about the Big Hill.

Her mother and father rarely talked about the Big Hill in front of her, and Jessie knew why. There wasn't another thing in the world they ever argued about, just the Big Hill. They would tease one another from time to time, but they would never really argue – not in Jessie's hearing anyway. They had spats of course, like anyone. Interrupt her father when he was making one of his 'creatures' in his shed and there was always trouble. But her mother never dug her heels in, never lost her temper, except when she was defending the Big Hill.

Catherine O'Malley – her mother's name before she married – was without doubt the most beautiful woman on the island, and therefore the cause of much admiration and envy. She had a mass of shining dark hair and eyes to match. Jessie knew the story well, and she loved to think of it, often. There was hardly a man who hadn't wanted to marry her mother. She was engaged to Michael Murphy, who owned the salmon farm now and the Big Hill too, when Jimmy Parsons, this 'blow-in' from England, this foreigner, this sculptor, came to stay for a summer holiday. He set eyes on Catherine O'Malley, took her fishing one day, married her and never went away.

Everyone knew Michael Murphy was still in high

dudgeon about it even all these years later. He was a squat little man and rich as Croesus – the very opposite of her father, who stood nearly two metres in his boots, and hadn't a penny to his name. He was almost always in his boots too, either out in the fields shepherding his flock or in his shed carving his beloved 'creatures' that no one ever seemed to want to buy. He didn't seem to mind too much, and Jessie didn't mind at all. They were like family to her. She had given every one of them a name, and when she was little he would tell her stories about them in the dark before she went off to sleep. Her father only took his boots off in the evenings and then his dirty toes would be sticking out of his socks, and he'd be scratching them. He wasn't perfect, but as a father he was a whole lot better than Michael Murphy would ever have been.

Jessie could picture them downstairs now as she listened to them. He'd be sitting in the rocker, Panda at his feet, and she'd be at the ironing.

'You haven't said much,' she heard him saying.

'Well, that's because there's not a lot to say.'

'You got to see the minister then, at the Dáil?'

'Yes.'

'Well?'

'Well, you'll be glad to hear that he agrees with you, you and all the others, all except old Mister Barney.'

'He said no then?'

'No, Jimmy. He said yes. He said yes to money, yes to destruction, yes to pollution. Oh, he's a real yes-man.'

'Well, you did what you could. No one could've done more, that's for sure. So if it's going to happen, best just to accept it, eh?'

'Never. Never. I'll never accept it. I was born here, remember? I grew up on that hill. I dreamed my dreams up there. The place is in my blood. And they want to send bulldozers to cut the top off my mountain, my hill, so that Michael Murphy and his kind can dig out the gold and get rich – as if they're not rich enough already. Well, they'll do it over my dead body. And I mean that.'

'Cath, for God's sake, why do you go on so? You've done what you can. Everyone respects you for it. I do, that's for sure. But this is the nineteen nineties we're living in. A hundred and fifty years ago there were over a thousand people living here on Clare, now there's barely a hundred and twenty. The way things are going, in ten years' time, there'll be half that. And why? Because there's no work here, no money. Bed and breakfast, a few tourists in the summer, sell a lobster or two, but that's it. There's nothing here for the young people to stay for. I don't like Michael Murphy any more than you do but, like him or not, at least he's brought work to the island. That gold mine will mean work for a generation or more, and money to develop the island.'

'Oh yes.' Her mother's blood was up now. 'And at what cost? We'll have streams of arsenic from the mine running down the hill, poisoning our children and our sheep – and that's what the experts said, not me. They're kicking old Mister Barney out of his shack, when the poor old man just wants to be left to finish his days in peace. And you know and I know that they won't employ islanders in the mine. They say they will, but they won't. People like that never do. They'll bring in outsiders, blow-ins.'

'I'm a blow-in, or had you forgotten?' said her father. There was a silence. 'Look, Cath,' he went on, 'in the last three years, ever since this thing started, we must have been through it a thousand times. You've made your point, you've argued your case. Your last chance was Dublin. You said so yourself, you said it was the last ditch. For goodness sake, even your own mother says you should give it up.'

'Don't you dare use my mother against me!' Her voice was sharp with anger. 'What's happened to you? You're supposed to be an artist, aren't you? A thinking man? Can you not see that it's against nature itself to cut the top off a mountain, any mountain, no matter where, just for a pot of stinking gold. All gold is fool's gold, don't you know that? You cut the top off the Big Hill, you dig out whatever's inside, and you suck out the soul of this place. There'll be nothing left. What'll it take to make you see it, Jimmy?' She cried then and Jessie could see in her mind's eye her father putting his arms round her and shushing her against his shoulder. 'I can't let them do it, Jimmy,' she wept. 'I won't.'

'I know, I know. But whatever happens, Cath, don't go hating me for what I think. I've been honest with you. I must be honest and say what I think, you know that. We've a whole life to lead here, Jess to look after, wood to sculpt and hundreds of silly sheep with their limping feet and their dirty little tails. We mustn't have this thing between us.' After that there was a lot of sniffling, and then subdued laughter.

'And talking of honesty, Jimmy Parsons.' It was her mother again, happier now, 'Jess tried the Big Hill again, didn't she? That's how she hurt herself, isn't it?'

'You can't stop her, Cath. And what's more I don't think we should. All right, so she fell over and hurt herself, but at least she tried. And if that's anyone's fault, it's yours. You were forever telling her, remember? "You can do it," you'd say. "You can do anything you want, if you want it badly enough. Forget about your lousy palsy."

Well, that's just what she's doing. She's set her heart on reaching the top of the Big Hill. She's a brave little heart and I'm not about to stop her from trying.'

'How far did she get?'

'To the top, of course. Doesn't she always? You know Jessie and her capacity for wishful thinking, for telling stories. But I think maybe she got a lot further up this time. She was so happy, so pleased with herself. Wouldn't it be just about the best thing in the world if she really made it, if one day she really made it right to the top of the Big Hill?'

'There you are then, Jimmy,' said her mother, so softly Jessie could scarcely hear, 'another reason if you ever needed one, and maybe the best reason, why the Big Hill has to be saved. Call it holy, call it magic, call it what you will, but there is something about that mountain, Jimmy. I can't describe it. I've been up there hundreds of times in my life and you know something? I've never once felt alone.'

Listening in her bed, turning her gold earring over and over in her hand, the indisputable evidence that she had indeed reached the summit of the Big Hill that afternoon, Jessie was tempted to go downstairs, burst into the kitchen and tell them the whole story from beginning to end: the climb, the voice, the earring, everything. She was boiling with indignation at her parents' disbelief, at their lack of faith. Yet she knew there was no point in protesting. She had been caught out often enough before, and by both of them too. She was a good storyteller, but a bad liar because she always went too far, became too fantastical.

Yes, she could dangle the earring in their faces, but what of the rest of the story? Why should they believe her just because she'd found an earring? And were they really likely to believe she had heard a voice, and had a conversation with someone who wasn't there? She wasn't even sure she believed it herself. She looked down at the only solid evidence she had. The earring was still wet from Barry's bowl, so she dried it on her nightie. Downstairs she could hear the television was on. The Big Hill argument was over, till the next time.

She climbed out of bed and sat down in front of her mirror. She held the ring up to her ear and turned sideways to look at herself in profile. She'd try it on. She'd had her ears pierced in Galway the year before. She took out her sleepers. It hurt a little, but she persevered through all the wincing until finally there it was, swinging from her lobe, glowing yellow-gold in the light.

'Perfect,' said a voice from behind her, the same voice

she'd heard up on the Big Hill. A warm shiver crawled up her back and lifted her hair on her neck. 'Pretty as a picture. It never looked half as good on me. Maybe one day I'll find you the other one for the other ear. I've got it somewhere. And by the way, who's that boy in the room next door?'

'My cousin Jack,' Jessie breathed. 'He's from America.'

'Well, now there's a thing,' came the voice again. 'America. I've been there, you know – a long while back, it's true, but I've been there. Maybe I'll tell you about it one day, when we know each other better.'

'I'm not going mad, am I?' Jessie said. 'You really are there, aren't you?' Jessie shivered. She was suddenly cold.

'Sure I am, Jessie,' said the voice, 'and you're not at all mad either, I promise you that. It's just that I want something done and I can't do it all on my own. I need help. I need a friend or two with a bit of spirit, if you see what I'm saying. In my experience, and I've had a fair bit of it in my time, you have to choose your friends very carefully.'

'But what do you need a friend for?'

'All in good time, Jessie.' The voice was fainter now. 'I'll be seeing you.'

For just a fleeting moment, there was a fading face in the mirror behind her. Jessie had the impression of a mass of dark dishevelled hair, radiant bright eyes and a ghost of a smile on the woman's face, not old exactly, not young either; somehow both at the same time. She turned around. The room was quite empty. She could feel there was no one there any more, but she knew for sure that there had been someone, and that whoever she was had gone. She had imagined none of it. She took the earring off, dropped it back into Barry's bowl and covered it over with the stones. She wiped her hand on her nightie and swung herself into bed.

From next door came a low rhythmic roar. It was some moments before Jessie worked out what it could be. Jack was snoring, just like Panda did, only louder. Suddenly the door opened and her mother stood there, silhouetted against the light.

'You awake still?'

'Yes, Mum.'

'How's the bump?'

'Fine.'

'Shall I give you a kiss goodnight?' Her mother sat down on the bed beside her and snuggled her close. 'Love you both, you know,' she whispered in her ear. 'But I'm not going to back down over the Big Hill. You understand that, don't you?'

'Course.'

She kissed her forehead and sat back up. 'And don't worry about Jack. He's a nice enough boy, you'll see. He's not had a happy time, y'know, what with his mother going off like she did, and now his dad not being well. Give him time, there's a girl.' She shivered, and looked around her. 'It's terrible cold in here,' she said. 'Have you had the window open or what?' Jessie shook her head. Her mother pulled the duvet up to her chin and stood up. 'Maybe it's a ghost then,' she laughed. 'Always cold, they say, when there's been ghosts about.'

Suddenly it occurred to Jessie that the face smiling down at her, her mother's face, was much like the face she had seen in the mirror. They smiled the same smile. They had the same hair, the same mouth even.

'You weren't in here a moment ago, were you, Mum?' she asked.

'No. Why?'

'Maybe I dreamed you,' said Jessie.

'Maybe you did. Sleep now.' And she went away, leaving Jessie alone in the dark. I *have* seen a ghost, Jessie thought. I *have* heard a ghost. I *have* felt the cold of a ghost. I should be frightened out of my skin, but I'm not. The snoring next door lulled her into a deep sleep.

Jessie and Jack were walking down the farm lane towards

school the next morning, Mole following along behind. 'You snore, do you know that?' Jessie said.

'I do not.'

'How do you know? If you're asleep you can't tell, can you? I heard you.'

'Well, at least I don't talk to myself.'

Jessie knew at once what he had overheard. 'Oh that. I was just talking to a ghost, wasn't I?' She said it half to tease, but half because she longed to tell someone, and she knew he wouldn't believe her. She was right.

He looked down at her and smiled. 'Oh yeah?'

Jessie shrugged her shoulders. 'You think what you like. I'm not bothered.' The school bell was ringing. 'Sometimes I think Mrs Burke's a ghost. She sort of floats, and she's always appearing suddenly out of nowhere.'

'Who's Mrs Burke?'

'She's my teacher, your teacher now, head teacher too; real old stick. Come on, we'll be late. And she eats you if you're late.' She looked up at him and smiled. 'Don't worry, you're too skinny for her. Mrs Burke, she likes little fat things like me.' When his smile opened, the sun glinted on his silver brace.

They hurried on, passing the abbey and the church, and then turning up the school lane towards the playground. It was ominously quiet, and Jessie soon saw why. The whole school was waiting for them, staring at them through the playground fence, all silent and wide-eyed.

'He's my cousin,' Jessie announced. 'He's called Jack and he's from America. And you can all stop your gawping, so you can.'

4 JAWS

'WELCOME TO OUR LITTLE SCHOOL, JACK.' MRS
Burke took her glasses off and laid them on her open
Bible, as she always did after morning prayers. 'I did
notice,' she went on, 'that there weren't that many eyes
closed during prayers this morning. Now I know that it's
a bit like having someone from another planet, but Jack is
only from the United States of America which is just a
little way across the ocean from here, that's all. There's
hardly one of us in this room who hasn't got an uncle over
there, or an aunty or a cousin or whatever. As you see,
they have two legs like we do, two arms, a couple of eyes
and they even speak the same sort of language, don't you,
Jack?' Jack tried to smile.

'So children, we will have no more of the staring, will we? It is not polite and not at all friendly either. Jack is here for our last few weeks of term, and then I believe into the summer holidays as well. So you'll see plenty of him. And we want him to have fond memories of Clare Island to take back home. So let's all of us show him just how friendly we can be, shall we?'

Liam Doherty took Mrs Burke at her word. In playtime, Liam made a beeline for Jack; and where Liam went, others soon followed. In no time at all, Jack found himself backed up against the playground fence being peppered with questions: about American football and baseball, about cowboys and cops. Liam asked if he could try on his baseball cap and Jack handed it over, a little reluctantly. It was passed around after that, but by the time the bell went for the end of playtime, he had it back again. By now he seemed to be enjoying all this new-found adulation, revelling in it almost, Jessie thought; and she was irritated by that.

Wherever he went, he seemed to be flanked by Liam Doherty and his gang. Marion Murphy seemed to have taken an instant shine to him as well, so she was never too far away either. Jessie kept her distance. Jack seemed to have forgotten that she even existed. For the rest of the day he hardly spoke to her, even at lunchtime. By the afternoon, Jessie was seething inside, and that made her written work even worse than usual.

Jessie was never much good anyway at her writing – that was why she hated doing it. Whatever she did, however hard she tried, her writing always came out all spindly and crooked. Everyone else could do it better, and faster too. Jessie's hands simply wouldn't do what her brain told them to do. And it wasn't just her hands that wouldn't obey her. It was her toes too. Whenever she tried to write, her toes would curl up under her feet and cramp themselves. She couldn't stop them. Mrs Burke came and bent over her to see how she was getting on.

'You're just going to have to try harder, aren't you, Jessie?' She'd said it often enough before, but it still hurt. 'I mean, just took at that writing. It's like a demented spider. I've told you till I'm blue in the face, hold your pencil this way, with the forefinger pressed down. You can grip it better.' How would she know what my hands can and can't do? Jessie thought. Doesn't she think I *want* to grip it better? 'Turn the page and try it again, Jessie.' Jessie sighed audibly, and with insolent intent. 'That'll be quite enough of that, Jessie Parsons. I'm not going to treat you any different from the others. It's no good you feeling sorry for yourself all your life.'

That was the moment when Jessie had finally had

enough. 'I do not feel sorry for myself, Miss,' she said, so fired up now that she could not stop herself. 'And you do treat me differently. You wouldn't take me up the Big Hill with the others, would you? You said I couldn't climb it. Well, I did. I climbed the Big Hill. I climbed it all by myself.'

'You did what?'

'I climbed it,' Jessie insisted.

Mrs Burke's furious frown lightened to a half-mocking smile. 'I don't think so, Jessie. I think what you mean to say is that you climbed it in your head. You always did have a powerful imagination. But what you mustn't do – and I've told you this before – is to confuse the one with the other, fact with fiction. Perhaps your father helped you up, gave you a piggyback, was that it?'

'I did it on my own,' Jessie said, her eyes fixed on Mrs Burke, the defiance quite undisguised, quite fearless.

'Jessie Parsons.' Mrs Burke looked down at her severely and arranged a wisp of grey hair behind her ear. 'What you are telling me is an untruth, a lie, and if I teach you just one thing before you leave this school it will be to tell the truth.' The class were all silent now, all watching. Mrs Burke went on, her voice thin with menace, 'You did *not* climb the Big Hill, and I won't have you say that you did. I won't have you use your disability as a weapon against the world, as an excuse for lying. You will write out fifty times, and neat, mind: "I did not climb the Big Hill." Is that quite clear and understood? You have one week. I'll not hear another word about it.'

There were lots of words about it, mostly from Marion Murphy, all of them disbelieving, most of them mocking. Jessie endured them all – it was the best way. Jack kept out of it and said nothing, until they were walking home together after school.

'Did you?' he asked suddenly.

'Did I what?'

'Did you climb that hill like you said?'

'If I say I did, I did,' Jessie snapped.

'All the way to the top?'

'Yes, and with these two legs,' Jessie said acidly. 'They're the only ones I've got.' They didn't speak for a moment or two.

'I brought my Rollerblades,' said Jack.

'So?'

'You want to try?'

Jessie smiled for the first time that day. 'All right,' she said, and they walked on for a while before she asked what she had been wanting to ask ever since she first saw him. 'What do you have all that steel in your mouth for?'

'Keeps my teeth straight,' Jack replied.

'I've got calipers. You know what calipers are?' Jack
didn't. 'Same as your thing, only for legs,' Jessie explained.
'I don't like them, so I don't put them on, unless I have to.
You know what Liam Doherty called you?'

'No.'

'Jaws,' she said, and he flashed his teeth at her and
laughed.

The rollerblading was not a great success, not for Jessie
anyway. They used the road at the end of the farm lane. It
was tarmac, and smooth enough in places; but there were
always a lot of pot-holes and bumps in the way, and, worst
of all, sheep droppings. Then there were sheep themselves
and Mole, loitering with intent, somehow always in the
way. For days and days she practised with Jack, but no
matter how hard she tried, the only way she could ever
stay upright was by hanging on to him. Whenever she let
go, she simply fell over. In the end she was forced just to
sit on the bank and watch him whizzing along the road,
gliding and weaving with consummate ease. It was not
doing much for Jessie's self-esteem, and anyway she had
her lines to do. Mrs Burke had given her a week. The week
was almost up and she hadn't even started yet. She left
him to it.

Later that evening, she was still at the kitchen table

writing her lines when she heard the tractor coming up the lane. Her mother came in, kicking off her boots, and washed her hands at the sink.

'Homework?' she said.

'Lines,' Jessie replied, curling her arm round to hide what she was writing.

'Why? What did you do?'

'Nothing. Just my writing wasn't good enough, that's all.' And she said no more about it.

'How many have you got to do?'

'Fifty.'

'That's nothing at all. It was always at least a hundred when I was at school.' Jessie felt like having a good rant about Mrs Burke, but there was no point. It wasn't only Mrs Burke who thought she was lying about the Big Hill, was it? Everyone did, even her own mother and father. They might pretend to believe her, to make her feel better, but they didn't. Besides, Jessie had learnt a long time ago that neither of them would hear a thing against Mrs Burke. So any troubles at school, she always kept to herself.

'Where's Jack?' her mother asked.

'Upstairs with his Walkman. He's got two Walkmen and three Game Boys. Are they made of money or what?'

'Your Uncle Sean's worked very hard for what he's got, Jess. That's maybe what's made him ill.'

'What's the matter with him?'

'He's ill, very ill. Let's just leave it at that, shall we?'

'Will he get better?'

'Yes,' she said quietly. 'God willing.' She put her arms round Jessie's neck and hugged her. 'You remember we've got to go out tonight, don't you? Island Meeting.'

'It'll be about the Big Hill again, I suppose,' Jessie sighed, and her mother moved away. 'Doesn't anybody talk about anything else around here?'

'Don't you care what happens to it, Jess?' said her mother, sitting down across the table from her.

'Of course I do, but why does everyone always have to shout about it? You and Dad, you go on and on. You never agree. No one ever agrees about it.'

'Sometimes, Jess, you've got to shout, else people just won't listen.' She leaned towards her and lifted her chin so that Jessie had to look into her eyes. 'And there's some things that are so important,' she said.

'Not that important,' Jessie replied. 'I don't like it when you and Dad shout; and besides, I don't know what the fuss is all about. The mining people, they've said they'll fix it afterwards, haven't they?'

'There's some things you just can't fix, Jess,' said her mother. 'It's like an egg. You cut the top off an egg, but you can't put it back on again, can you?'

'Well, I'm not getting into your silly arguments,' Jessie shouted, throwing down her pencil. The tears came into her eyes. 'You see? As soon as you start talking about it, we start shouting.'

Jack was standing at the door, pale and distraught. He looked from one to the other.

'It's gone,' he said. 'I looked all over. I've lost it.'

'What is it, Jack?' Jessie's mother went over to him.

'My lucky arrowhead. It was in my coat pocket, and now it's gone.'

'We'll find it, Jack,' said Jessie's mother. 'Don't worry. It's got to be somewhere, hasn't it?'

'I never go anywhere without it,' said Jack. 'It brings me luck.' And Jessie saw then that his eyes were red with crying. 'If I don't find it, my luck's gone for good. I know it is.'

'We'll find it,' said Jessie's mother. 'It'll turn up, you'll see. Now, how about some nice soda bread and honey. You like honey? We've got the best honey in all of Ireland. Will you try some?'

Jack did like the honey, just so long as it was spread on top of peanut butter. It was about the first thing he had liked in all the time he'd been with them. Jessie looked on in awe as he ate four whole slices and then washed it all down with Coke. He seemed a lot happier after that. They turned Jack's room inside out looking for his arrowhead, searched through every drawer, through every pocket. It was nowhere. They went up and down the road where they had been rollerblading. Nothing. Then it came on to rain and they had to go in.

'Tomorrow,' said Jessie's mother. 'We'll look again tomorrow. I've got to get ready for the meeting.'

That evening, Jack and Jessie were left on their own, with peanut butter and honey sandwiches for their supper. Jessie didn't like to admit it, but she'd taken quite a liking to them. She was eating them at the same time as she did her lines. The television was on in the corner. It was football again, or 'soccer', as Jack insisted on calling it. Jessie was suddenly aware that Jack was looking over her shoulder. 'You left a word out,' he said, pointing. 'It says, "I *did* climb the Big Hill." '

'I told you, I did,' said Jessie.

'I know, but Mrs Burke said . . .'

'I don't care what Mrs Burke said. I've done lines for her before, hundreds of them. She won't read it anyway – she never does – and I'm not going to write it when it's not true. I climbed that hill and I'm not saying I didn't, not for her, not for anyone.'

Jack grinned broadly. 'My dad would say you've got guts.'

'Are you very rich?' Jessie asked.

Jack looked at her for a moment. 'Yeah,' he said. 'I guess you could say we've got pretty much everything you'd want. Two houses, one on Long Island and a farm up in Vermont. Two yachts, three cars. Rich enough, I guess.'

'Three cars? What d'you want three cars for?'

'Well, maybe two, and the VW Beetle I work on. I love engines.'

'Your father, Uncle Sean, how come he's got so much money?'

Jack shrugged. 'I don't know. He just makes it. Like he says, he makes money make money. Doesn't tell me a lot about it. He's great. He takes me places – hunting, skiing, all that. Just the two of us.'

'What about your mum?' She knew she shouldn't have asked it, and she was relieved when Jack didn't seem upset.

'I don't see her any more,' he said quietly. 'Dad says it's best that way. Guess he's right too. They were always at each other's throats, shouting and stuff.' She wanted to ask him about how ill Uncle Sean was, but she didn't know how to. 'All that shouting about the Big Hill, a few nights back,' Jack went on, 'what was that all about?'

'You heard it?'

'And Marion Murphy at school. She kept going on about it, too.'

'She would be,' said Jessie. 'It's the lousy gold mine. You've got those who want it and you've got those who don't – not many now – in fact, just Mum and old Mister Barney. Marion's dad, Mr Murphy – he's the one that got it all going – well, he owns the Big Hill, and he's told everyone it'll mean lots of jobs and lots of money for the island. He's persuaded just about everyone now, even my dad. Tonight it's the final meeting, the last vote. Mum knows she'll lose, but she still won't give in. She says it's wrong. Dad says it's right. That's why they were shouting.'

'There was a lot of that back home,' said Jack, 'shouting I mean, Mom at Dad, Dad at Mom. And after that, they wouldn't even talk. Then Mom just left.' He was looking at her steadily, almost as if it were a warning.

Jessie was up in bed, and still thinking about what Jack had said, when she heard Clatterbang pull up outside. Panda was scrabbling at the door to get in, and then he was charging around downstairs like a wild thing. She heard a tap running in the kitchen and the kettle going on.

Her father was doing the talking. 'Well, maybe they won't find enough gold to make it worth their while.'

'But the damage will be done by then, won't it?' came the reply. 'Either way, they've still got to take the top off the hill to find out. But anyway, that's hardly the point is it? You voted against me, in public, and for everyone to see. Only Mister Barney stood up for the hill, Mister Barney and me. And what did that Michael Murphy say? That Mister Barney was objecting out of self-interest, just because he was going to have to move house, and how the mining company had laid on such a wonderful house for him to move into. "A minor inconvenience," he called it. Poor dear Mister Barney. And did you speak up for him? No. Did you speak up for me? No. I feel like you stabbed me in the heart, Jimmy. That's what I feel.'

Jessie pulled the duvet up over her head and clamped a pillow round her ears. She wanted to hear no more. She didn't want to think about it, but she couldn't help herself. She was wondering what would happen to her if they split up like Jack's mother and father had, about which of them she would be left with. She'd have more fun with her father. He could at least forget about her lousy palsy and treat her straight. She loved him for that. But then he never cuddled her that much. Her mother did. When she was in real trouble, it was always to her mother that she went. She'd cry up against her softness and her mother would smooth her hair, and Jessie loved her for that. She was crying now and trying not to because she didn't want them to hear. She heard a knock and her door opening. She pushed back her duvet. Jack was standing in the doorway.

'I was thinking,' he said slowly. 'You're going to get in real trouble about those lines.' He came further into the room. 'Something the matter?'

'No.'

'Well, I was thinking. If Mrs Burke does read those lines and you get in more trouble, then maybe you could prove it to her, and to all the kids in school.'

'How do you mean?'

'How'd it be if I got some of the guys, Liam Doherty and the others, and we all went up the Big Hill with you, and then we told Mrs Burke? She'd have to believe us, right? How about it? Would you do it?'

'Course I would.' Jessie spoke without really thinking. It seemed to her this was like a challenge, that maybe Jack didn't believe her either. But when she did think about it, she immediately began to regret it. Just because she had climbed the Big Hill once, it didn't mean she could do it again.

'Anyway,' she said, 'if she doesn't read them, and she won't, then I won't have to do it, will I?' She just hoped she was right.

'Your mom lost her vote?' Jack went on.

She nodded. 'See you,' he said, and then he went out.

Jessie couldn't sleep that night, and it wasn't just the owl outside. Her head swarmed with endless puzzlements and debates and anxieties. Was Jack right about the shouting? Would it just get worse until they split up? Should she put in the one word in her lines that would make life easier at school tomorrow? If she did, and Mrs Burke did read them, then at least she wouldn't have to climb the Big Hill again. And what would happen if she tried to climb the Big Hill in front of everyone, and then failed? She'd never live it down. Marion Murphy wouldn't let her. And that was another thing. Marion Murphy was hovering around Jack a lot too close, and she didn't like it. She didn't like it one bit.

She got out of bed and went to watch Barry for a while. He was asleep at the bottom of his bowl, just breathing, nothing else. It was as much to wake him up as anything that she put her hand in and fished around in the stones for the earring. She took it out and shook it dry. And what of the voice she had heard on the Big Hill? Was it real or imagined? What of the face in the mirror and the earring in her hand? What *was* going on? Her feet were getting cold, so she hid the earring deep in the stones again, said goodnight to Barry, and went back to bed.

The moon lit her room and the shadows from the tree danced across the ceiling above her head. 'Are you there?' she whispered. 'Can you hear me?' The owl answered from the abbey tower. 'Bog off,' she said. 'I wasn't talking to you.'

But as she drifted into sleep at last, watching the moving shadows, she fancied they were not shadows any more, but waves. Dipping through the waves came a galley and on the prow of the galley stood a woman, her hair flying out in the wind, her cloak whipping about her shoulders, a flag fluttering over her head, a flag with a red pig emblazoned on it. Then the woman was looking down at her from the ceiling and smiling at her. 'It's late, Jessie,' she was saying. 'Just you go to sleep now, and let tomorrow take care of itself. It always does.'

6 THE GHOST OF GRANIA O'MALLEY

TRUE ENOUGH, TOMORROW DID TAKE CARE OF itself. Mrs Burke remembered the week was up and asked for the lines. As expected and hoped for, she gave them no more than a cursory glance and dropped them into her waste-paper bin. 'No more of your nonsense now, Jessie,' she said, and that was that. Jessie looked across at Jack and smiled her relief. So she wouldn't have to prove it, she wouldn't have to climb the Big Hill again after all. For Jessie, school that day was one long sigh of relief.

Jack's rollerblades made him, without any question, the most popular person the school had ever known. Jessie sat on her place on the wall and watched him, her legs swinging. She felt real pride that Jack was a cousin of hers. She was less pleased when Marion contrived to have more turns than anyone else, and somehow she always seemed to need Jack to help her up when she fell over. Miss Jefferson had a try too, and she was quite good. Jack showed her what to do and stood back. She wobbled just once across the playground, and everyone cheered and clapped, even Mrs Burke. It seemed to set her in a good mood for the rest of the day.

That afternoon they all did a comparative study of Clare Island, County Mayo, Ireland, and Long Island, New York, U.S.A. – the one barely four miles long, the other over a hundred; the one you could only get to by ferry, the other with a road and rail link to and from New York; the one inhabited until four hundred years before by Red Indians (Jack said they were called 'Native Americans', not 'Indians'), and the other the last stronghold of the Irish-Gaelic tribes against the Normans and the English.

Then Liam Doherty was asked to stand up and explain the rules of Gaelic football, and Jack had to say how American football was different. Jessie was bored by all this, for there seemed to her to be very little difference between the two. The goalposts were about the same shape and, to her, it was just a lot of people running around kicking a ball and shouting, and not very interesting at all. The Americans wore funny helmets and dressed up like mutant giants and the Irish didn't – for her that was the only difference. Liam was becoming a little edgy because people weren't as interested in what he was saying – mostly because they knew it already – as they were in what Jack was saying.

Mrs Burke finished off the whole day by telling them all what both Irish and American had in common, Clare Islanders and Long Islanders. 'The main thing is,' she said, 'that we speak the same language, and that's good, because it means we can understand one another better. We are both free countries and democracies, and we've that to be thankful for. Do you know what a democracy is?' No one answered. 'Well, it means that we Irish vote for what we want; and so do you Americans, don't you, Jack?'

'I guess,' said Jack.

'Take for instance, last night,' Mrs Burke went on, 'when we had our Island Meeting. A perfect example of democracy in action. Almost everyone was for the gold mine, and just two were against. So like it or not, the gold mine is coming. No one can stop it now. That's the power of democracy for you.'

Jessie could not leave it like that. She had to speak up, she had to defend her mother. Her anger made her suddenly brave. She put her hand up.

'Yes, Jessie?' said Mrs Burke.

'My mother says that voting is all very well, Miss, but just because a thing is popular, she says that doesn't make it right. She doesn't think the gold mine is right, and neither does old Mister Barney.'

Mrs Burke glowered at her for a moment over the top of her glasses and then looked up at the school clock. 'I think that'll be all for today,' she said. 'Tidy your tables, children.'

They were in the playground at the end of school, shrugging on coats when the skirmishing began. It was Marion Murphy that started it all. She sauntered up to Jessie with that lipcurl of a smile on her face, the smile that Jessie always knew meant trouble. She was a head taller than Jessie and big all over, a great round face and a mouth to match.

'Your mum,' she said, 'is she mad in the head, or what? My mum says that your mum just likes the men to look at her – that's why she gets up and talks like she does. A bit of tart, my mum says. Married a lousy blow-in too.'

'You've a filthy mouth on you, Marion Murphy,' Jessie said, fixing her with her most contemptuous and withering stare. But the sneer on Marion's face was still there, so Jessie had to go on, 'My mum's got a perfect right to say what she thinks about the Big Hill – and besides, she's right and the rest of you's wrong. You *shouldn't* go cutting the tops off mountains just for a lump of gold, and they *will* poison the water like she says, and there *won't* be work for everyone either, and they *won't* put it all back as good as new when they've finished, like your daft daddy says. It's all lies. And if the men look at my mum, that's because she's beautiful, and if they don't look at your mum, that's because she's an ugly old cow.'

She had gone too far. She knew it, but she just could not rein herself in. She was trembling with fury, and with fear too. She was probably safe enough from physical attack – there were some advantages to being the way she was. And anyway, Marion was all mouth – she hoped. There was a crowd closing in round them now, almost the whole school. Jessie was glad to find Jack there beside her.

Marion's face was scarlet. 'Cripple!' she screamed at her. 'You're just a cripple, you know that, just a cripple. My mum says you shouldn't be allowed in the same school with us. They should send you away so's no one's got to look at you.'

Jessie had never liked Marion, and she knew Marion had never liked her, but she'd never said such a thing before. No one had. They might have thought it. Jessie had often caught sight of a side-glance here, a lowering of the eyes there, and she knew what they meant well enough, but it had never been spoken out loud before. It was suddenly out in the open, and the shock of it took her breath away. She was stunned to silence. Jack spoke up.

'We're going home,' he said, taking her elbow. The crowd parted for them and seemed a little disappointed it had come to no more than harsh words.

'I hate her, I really hate her,' Jessie said much later, as they walked away past the abbey ruins. The post van came down the hill past them. Mrs O'Leary, postlady and pubkeeper, waved at them cheerily.

'What's a blow-in?' Jack asked. 'Marion said your pa was a blow-in.'

'Someone like you – foreigner, English, Irish, no matter what. If you weren't born here, you're a blow-in.'

'So?' said Jack. 'Back home, that would make just about everyone a blow-in. Well, maybe not the Native Americans, but even they probably blew in from somewhere, I guess.' They walked on for a while in silence.

'D'you find your lucky arrowhead yet?' Jessie asked.

Jack shook his head. 'Maybe it wasn't that lucky anyway,' he said. He stopped suddenly. 'Hey, listen. You want to take me up this hill of yours?' he asked. 'You want to take me up the Big Hill?' It took Jessie by surprise.

'What, now?'

'Why not? You've done it before, haven't you?' he said. 'I'll tell the guys afterwards. How about it?'

'I don't want you to tell them,' she said. 'I don't care if they believe me or not. Don't care if no one believes me.'

'I believe you,' Jack said. 'I just want to go up there, OK? I've got to find out what all the fuss is about, that's all.'

'OK,' said Jessie, but she meant more than that. She meant: 'Thanks, thanks for believing in me.' She gave him a smile to tell him so, and then immediately began to worry whether she would be able to make it to the top again. She had no choice but to try. There was no way out of it.

They had to go past the end of the farm lane to get to the Big Hill. Mole was grazing the grass verge and followed them. By the time they reached the grassy clearing by Mister Barney's shack, Panda was there too, bounding away into the bracken after rabbits, his tail whirling. Jessie was counting out her rhythm in her head: one and two, one and two, one and two. She hadn't the breath to talk. Having Jack alongside made it easier in one way, but more difficult in another. It was easier because she knew he'd be there to help her if she tumbled, but more difficult because she knew he'd never believe her ever again if she failed to reach the top.

When they got to the stream across the path, Jack sat down on a rock for a breather, wiping the sweat from his face. 'We're only halfway up,' she said, tottering on past him, 'so we're neither up nor down. What's keeping you?' Seeing him sitting there exhausted, made her feel good, very good; but she felt even better still when she reached the gulley beyond the waterfall, and could see the summit up there ahead of her. But then, without warning, she sat down with a bump and Jack was crouching beside her.

'You OK?'

'I need a hand up, that's all.' He helped her up and steadied her. 'I'm fine,' she said. 'Fine.' From now on it simply did not occur to her that she might not reach the top. She sat down only once more, more awkwardly this time, and fell sideways into the undergrowth. Jack hauled her on to her feet again and freed her from a bramble that was caught in her hair.

'Almost there,' he said; and they were too. They were calling out the rhythm together now: 'One and two, one and two, one and two.' A last scramble over rocks on hands and knees, and then they were stretched out on a great soft cushion of pink thrift at the summit, their eyes closed against the sun. After a while Jessie propped herself up on her elbows. Jack was standing on the highest rock and gazing out to sea.

'Your mom's right, Jess,' he said. No one ever called her Jess, except her mother and father, but Jessie found she didn't mind at all. In fact, she liked it. 'They shouldn't do it,' he went on. 'They shouldn't go cutting the top off. I don't care how much gold there is inside here. I never saw anything like this place. It's really special, you know that? If we let them knock it down, then no one's ever going to stand here like I am and look at this. All you get from gold is money. Money sure makes you rich, but rich doesn't make you happy. This makes you happy.'

'You on Mum's side then?'

'I guess I am. What about you?'

Jessie was looking around her. Jack was right. It *was* special. It *was* beautiful. It was the *perfect* place. 'I don't think I ever really made up my mind about it until now,' she said, 'until right now. But yes, I am on Mum's side, and not just because of what Marion said either. Mum's right. She's been right all along.' She tried to get up, but found it difficult. He came over and helped her to her feet. 'Anyway,' Jessie said, 'it doesn't matter any more. It's too late, it's all decided.'

The sunlight danced over the rock pool and seemed to

be inviting them to drink. Jack was there before she was. He cupped his hands under the spring, caught the water and drank it. Jessie tried it the same way too, but could not keep her fingers tight enough together to hold the water. So she knelt down and put her mouth to the surface of the pool, as she had the last time she was up there. She drank long and deep, her eyes closed until she'd had enough. She wiped her mouth and watched the reflected clouds moving across the pool. She was remembering the earring and how she had found it there before. And then she knew she wasn't remembering it at all, she was looking directly at it. It was there, right in front of her eyes, lying at the bottom of the pool. It was like an echo in her mind, this feeling of having been somewhere before and then the same thing happening, in exactly the same place and in exactly the same way, like a dream, only clearer, more real. She reached down into the water, shattering the clouds, but Jack's hand was quicker than hers.

'Jeez, what's this?' he said, dangling the earring in front of her eyes.

'What does it look like?' a voice spoke from behind them, a voice Jessie recognised at once. 'You'll be needing the pair, I thought.' They turned. She was the woman from the mirror. She was the woman from Jessie's dream.

And she was here and now and barefoot on the rock, her hair all about her face.

'Well, have you no manners at all?' she said. 'You're gawping at me like a pair of gasping salmon. Look around you. It's just like you said, Jack. Isn't this the most perfect place in the entire world? My mountain this, my hill. I fought for it, we all did. We spilled good red Irish blood for it, and I'll not let them do it. I won't. But I'll need help.' And then to Jack: 'That was a fine speech you made. Did you mean it?' Jack nodded, backing away now and taking Jessie with him.

'Now where do you think you're going to?' She sprang down off the rock, lithe like a tiger, a sword hanging from her broad leather belt. She was about Jessie's mother's age, a little older perhaps and certainly stronger. There was a wild and weather-beaten look about her. 'Would I hurt you? Would I? Haven't I just given you my own earrings? Gold they are, Spanish gold. I filched them myself from the wreck of the *Santa Felicia*, a great Armada galleon that washed itself up on our rocks – a while ago now. And there's a whole lot more where they came from, my life's winnings you might say – or what's left of them anyway.'

She drew her sword and flourished it at the sea. 'These are my waters. You sail in my waters and you pay your dues. I took from anyone who came by, English, Spanish, Portuguese – all the same to me, all perfectly fair and square and above board. But if they didn't pay, well then, I took what was mine. Wouldn't you? A poor pirate's got to earn her crust somehow. How else is she to live into her old age? Tell me that if you will.'

Jessie sat down because she had to, because her legs wanted her to. It could not be what Jessie was thinking, because what she was thinking was impossible; but then maybe she had to believe the impossible might just be possible after all. The woman now striding towards her said she was a pirate, that the Big Hill was her mountain. It could be no one else. It had to be ... but then it couldn't be. She had been buried in the abbey hundreds of years ago. Jessie had seen the gravestone. They had read about her at school, the Pirate Queen of Clare Island. Mrs O'Leary's pub down by the quay was named after her.

Jessie screwed up all her courage, and then spoke. 'You're not ... you're not Grania O'Malley, are you?'

'And who else would I be?' she said.

6 GONE FISHING

THEY WERE ALONE AGAIN ON THE HILL. IT WAS as if time had stood still, and they had just rejoined it. For some moments they simply stood and stared at each other. Then Jack looked down at his hand. 'It's gone. I had it. I had the earring,' he whispered. 'I found it in the pool, didn't I?' Jessie nodded. 'And she *was* here, wasn't she? I wasn't dreaming it?' He didn't wait for an answer. 'Let's get out of here,' he said.

Mole wouldn't be caught, so Jack had to give Jessie a piggyback all the way down the hill. They reached the bottom in time to help Jessie's father drive the sheep along the road into the barn. They would be shearing the next day, he said, and it felt like rain. The fleeces had to be dry, so it was best to keep the sheep in overnight.

That evening the thunder rolled in from the sea and clattered around the island, and the rain fell hard and straight in huge drops that drummed incessantly on the tin roof of the kitchen. Inside, there was an unnatural silence over the supper table. Jessie's mother and father weren't speaking. She looked from one to the other willing them to talk, but neither did. It was just as Jack had said, first the shouting, then the silences.

Jack ate his peanut butter sandwiches ravenously and scarcely looked up. He seemed all wrapped up inside himself. Jessie longed to talk to him about everything that had happened up on the Big Hill, but there was never an opportunity to be alone together. He went up to bed early, and Jessie was about to follow him upstairs when her father asked her to help him check the sheep. 'Two pairs of eyes are always better than one,' he said.

The sheep filled the barn from wall to wall. Every one of them was lying down, except for one in the corner. 'I thought as much. She's lambing. She shouldn't be, but she is. That old ram must have got out again,' he said. 'She's only young. I think she'll need a hand. Do you want to do it?' Jessie had never told her father that she didn't like doing it. It was all the slime and the blood; and worst of all, the possibility that the lamb might be dead. She pretended. She had always pretended, and she pretended again now. Her father knelt down, holding the sheep on her side. Jessie found the feet inside and felt for the head. The lamb was alive. She tugged and her hands slipped. The little black feet were sucked back inside. She tried again. The lamb came out at the third pull and lay there, steaming and exhausted, on the ground. They sat watching the ewe for a while as she licked over her lamb, her eyes wary.

'Something the matter with Jack, is there?' her father asked suddenly.

'Not as far as I know. He can't find his lucky arrowhead, that's all.'

She had never before found it difficult to talk to her father, but then she'd never before wanted to ask him about such a thing. She wanted to ask him outright: 'Are you and Mum going to split up?' Then it occurred to her that maybe just by asking, just to speak of it, might make it more likely to happen.

'Come on, Jess,' he said, 'what's up?'

Luckily, there was something else troubling her, something she was longing to talk about to someone.

'I think I've seen a ghost, Dad.'

He looked down at her and laughed. 'Have you been at my whisky, Jess?'

'Course not.'

'You're serious, aren't you?'

'I've seen her in my mirror, Dad, and I heard her up on the Big Hill. Then today, this afternoon, I saw her. I really saw her. Honest, up at the top of the Big Hill.'

'At the top of the Big Hill, you say,' said her father, getting to his feet and brushing himself down. 'Now there's a thing.' He smiled down at her and helped her. 'D'you know, Jess, you go on like this and you'll make a writer one day. All the best writers don't know where the truth begins or where it ends. They're not liars at all, they're just dreamers. Nothing wrong with dreaming.' He pulled some straw out of her hair and let it fall to the ground. 'And by the by, don't you worry about your mother and me. It's the Big Hill. It's only the Big Hill that's between us. Once the mining's begun and there's nothing more to be done about it, then we'll be fine, you'll see.' Jessie felt a surge of relief coursing through her and warming her like sunshine. It didn't matter that he hadn't believed her ghost story. It didn't matter at all.

'Your hands are disgusting,' he said, and she wriggled her fingers in his face and giggled.

The weekend was spent shearing the sheep, all four of them together in the barn: her father pouring sweat as he bent over the sheep, her mother and Jack rolling the fleeces into bundles and sweeping up, while Jessie opened and shut the gate and drove the sheep into the shearing pen. Jack took to the shepherding as if he had been doing it all his life. Through it all, Jessie's mother and father scarcely spoke. Liam called in on Sunday morning after Mass. Marion Murphy had found a baseball bat, he said. Her father had brought it back from Miami on one of his trips. She'd lend it if she could play too. 'You could teach us,' said Liam. 'I've got a tennis ball. Five o'clock at the field. Will you come?'

Jessie went with him that evening, not because she had the slightest interest in baseball, but because at last she'd have a chance to talk to Jack about Grania O'Malley. All they had been able to do since they had met her was to exchange conspiratorial glances. They sauntered along the farm lane, side-stepping the puddles, Mole following along behind. Jack did all the talking.

'Jess, I've been thinking. About her, I mean, about what happened up there. Here's what I remember, or what I think I remember. We got to the top, right? We found the earring in the pool. I had it in my hand. Then out of nowhere comes this weird lady, kind of like a gypsy. She said she was a pirate, right? And she had a sword. She kept telling us all about the gold she'd taken off some ship, a Spanish ship, wasn't it? And her hair was black and curling down to her shoulders. I mean, I can see her like she was here right now. I didn't make this up, did I? You saw her too, right?' Jessie tried to answer, but Jack wouldn't let her.

'Now, we've got two choices. Either the whole thing was some fantastic dream, and we just dreamed the same dream – or it really happened. I don't reckon two people *can* dream the same dream. So, it happened, and if it happened, then we really met a ghost up there. Right? But there's something I can't figure out. It seemed like she knew you somehow, like she'd given you an earring before.'

'That's because she did,' said Jessie. 'I've seen her before. She came to my room. And she talked to me, on the Big Hill, the day you came. That's when I found the first earring. In the same pool. I keep it in Barry's bowl. But I didn't know who she was.'

'Something O'Malley, wasn't it?' said Jack.

'*Grania* O'Malley,' she said and Jack looked at her blankly. 'Don't you know who she is? She's in the history books. She was a terrible woman, a sort of pirate queen. She'd slit your throat as soon as look at you. Mrs Burke says she was a wicked scarlet woman. She had as many husbands as she had children, and sometimes they weren't husbands at all. But what I don't understand is the earring, the second earring. If she really was there, if it wasn't a dream, then where's the second earring? You had it in your hand.'

Then Liam and the others came along on their bikes and walked with them down towards the field. There could be no more talk of Grania O'Malley's ghost or the missing earring.

Baseball was like rounders, Jessie thought, except you wound yourself up into a frenzy before you threw the ball, the bat was a lot longer and, for some reason she didn't quite understand, the batter always got to wear Jack's baseball hat. She kept her distance. It wasn't the kind of game she could play very well. When they picked sides, she would be the last to be chosen and she always hated that. And besides, she didn't want to encounter Marion Murphy again. She'd sit it out.

Watching from the seat under the tree, with Mole grazing around her feet, Jessie could think of nothing else except the ghost on the Big Hill. Even when her legs cramped up with the cold and she had to rub the life back into them, she hardly felt the accustomed pain. There was still this niggling doubt in her mind. One way or another she had to know for sure. Perhaps the ghost was close by somewhere, watching, listening, just invisible, that's all. 'You're there, aren't you?' She said it aloud. 'Grania O'Malley, can you hear me? If you can hear me, let me see you, *please.*' The ball came rolling towards her feet, chased by Marion.

'Talking to yourself again?' said Marion, bending down to pick it up.

'No, I'm not,' she replied. Marion gave her a puzzled look, threw the ball in and ran off.

With each day that passed, and with no sign of the ghost, no reappearance, and no second earring, the two began to believe that they must have had some kind of joint hallucination. They went over it again and again, and both clearly remembered every little detail – or they thought they did. Jessie showed Jack the evidence of her first meeting with Grania O'Malley. Time after time she took the earring out of its hiding place in Barry's bowl and showed it to him, and each time Jack was even more sure it was the same as the one he'd had in his hand that afternoon on the Big Hill, quite sure, he said. She showed him the mirror where she'd seen the head of the ghost all those weeks before, and he sat in front of it just as she had, holding the earring in his hand, and looked deep into the mirror. 'And she was right behind you?' he said.

'Not all of her, just her head. But it was the same woman. It was Grania O'Malley. Honest it was.'

'But if we saw her like we think we did,' Jack went on, 'then where's the other earring?' That was always the problem they came back to. There *was* no second earring, and until there was a second earring, then there was room for doubt. They searched everywhere, everywhere they had looked for Jack's lucky arrowhead, and elsewhere too. But they found neither the second earring nor the lucky arrowhead.

Their shared doubts and fears threw them more and more together in school, as well as out of school too. In school, all the playground talk was of the controversy still raging over the Big Hill. Anyone who said a word against the gold mine was branded at once as some kind of traitor. So no one spoke up against the mine, except Jessie; and the more she found herself standing up for the preservation of the Big Hill, the surer she was of her cause. And being alone against the others only made her more defiant, more determined. Jack was her sole ally, but a silent one. He rarely left her side, and was, Jessie thought, the main reason anyone listened to her without shouting her down.

Jack was still new enough to fascinate. Baseball had become all the rage – every evening down on the field. Anyone who was anyone had by now acquired a baseball hat of sorts. He had a quiet way with him that everyone liked and respected. Marion Murphy, and she wasn't alone, still hung around him all she could. Jessie overheard her one rainy playtime when they were cooped up inside. 'I can't understand it,' Marion was saying. 'He's Jessie's cousin, and I fancy him rotten.'

It was Marion too who did most to stoke up the furore about the Big Hill. She would do all she could to provoke frequent and often nasty confrontations with Jessie. She'd catch her alone in the playground with her back to the fence so she couldn't get away, and she'd start yelling at her, nose to nose. Jack would intervene, always just in time. 'Getting mad won't help,' he'd say. 'Let's just cool it.' And Marion would back off, just like that. He had a way with Marion that no one else had.

But Jack couldn't be with Jessie all the time. It was the end of school one afternoon, and it was hot. Jessie was tired. Her legs had been hurting all day, and she just wanted to go home. Suddenly they were all around her, Marion Murphy and her pack. They were on about the Big Hill again and how Jessie's mother was the only one against it. She felt battered and bruised by their angry, scathing looks and their vicious words. She just wanted to run. But there was no way out. Suddenly, inexplicably, she felt a new power, a new courage rising within her, a new kind of strength; and she knew as she spoke, that the words that came out were not hers. She had become the face in the mirror, the voice on the Big Hill. She knew it was Grania O'Malley talking through her, she was quite sure of it. Where else could she have found the nerve? The words flowed out fluently, without her even having to think about them.

'Will you let me speak or not?' She waited till they were quiet, and then went on. 'Let's say you get your share of the gold – which you won't – what will you do with it? You can't eat it, you can't drink it.'

'Get rich, stupid!' Marion Murphy shouted into her face, and they all roared their support.

'Oh yes?' Jessie was quite undaunted. 'And meanwhile, they'll have torn a great hole in the Big Hill with their machines, so none of us will ever be able to stand up there again and look out to the Islands in Clew Bay. You'd like that, would you? Oh, and of course Mister Barney's in the way, isn't he? So we'll just kick him out and move him on. No problem. And the water in the wells will all be poisoned. But who cares? It won't matter, will it, because we'll all of us be eating off solid gold plates, and that'll make us as happy as pie, won't it? That hill has been there, Marion Murphy, since the beginning of time. Didn't St Patrick himself pray on it? Didn't Grania O'Malley keep watch on it against the English?'

Before the words came out, Jessie had never even known that St Patrick had prayed on the Big Hill, nor that Grania O'Malley had kept watch on it. Her speech silenced them, but only for a few moments. Then Marion was railing again. 'Don't listen to her. It's a lot of bull. Stuff St Patrick. Stuff Grania O'Malley. It'll be jobs for everyone, money for everyone – that's what my dad says. And anyway, it doesn't matter what you say, or your stupid mum says, 'cos she can't stop it now and neither can you. They're coming. The bulldozers are coming. What are you going to do, ask them nicely to stop?'

There was no way out for Jessie. She was in too deep to back away now. 'I'll lie down in front of them,' Jess said quietly. 'You see if I don't.' They all scoffed at her, hurled a few more insults, and at last went away and left her in peace.

She told Jack about it afterwards, when they were alone. 'You wouldn't really do it though, would you?' he said.

'If I have to. If I have to, I will. Now I've said it, I've got to, haven't I?'

'Then we'll do it together,' he said firmly.

'Honest?'

'We're family, right?'

It was that evening that Jessie and her mother found the newborn lamb dead beside the ruined cottage in the bog-oak field, the ewe still nuzzling it. The lamb was covered in black flies. 'Poor thing,' said her mother, waving the flies away. 'Born at the wrong time and in the wrong place. Bit like me, I think.' They dug a hole in the corner of the field, laid the lamb out and covered it up. Jessie looked away. She saw tears in her mother's eyes, but she said nothing. 'I saw Liam's mum. She told me about school,' said her mother, as they walked away.

'What about it?'

'About you, about Marion Murphy, about lying down in front of the machines when they come.'

'Jack says he'll do it with me,' said Jessie.

'Did he now? Well, he's a fine boy. I like him more every day, and so does your dad, but no one's going to lie down in front of anything. No one's going to get hurt. I'll find a way without that. I'm not going to give up, that's for sure.' They walked on in silence for a while. 'I'm so proud of you, Jess, you know that?' she said. 'So pleased you're on my side.'

'What about Dad?'

'Oh, he'll come round.' She smiled and put her arm round Jessie's shoulders. 'Give him time.'

'Only if you talk to him, Mum,' said Jessie. 'You've got to talk. Jack's mum and dad – he says it all started with shouting first of all, and then no one talked. And she just went off.'

'Listen, Jess, I'm not leaving. And your dad's not leaving either. He's dug his heels in over this, and so have I, that's all. We're both just doing what we think is right. I don't love him any the less, I promise. What he doesn't seem to understand just yet, is that I'm right. He still thinks he is. I have to persuade him that he's wrong, and that's never easy with anyone. I can promise you this though, Jess: there'll be no blood on the carpet when it's over. Believe me?'

Jessie said she did, but there was still an aching worry inside her that would not go away.

Jack came back at dusk, happy as a sandboy. He'd spent half the day with his head and hands deep inside Clatterbang's engine, and the rest of the time he'd been coaching the 'Pirates' – that was what the Clare Island baseball team now grandly called themselves. He was full of smiles as he threw himself breathless on to the sofa. 'The guys want some gloves and a real ball. I'm going to get Dad to send them over. They want Yankee caps like mine, too. What do you think? Can I call home?'

When he came back into the room some minutes later, all the light had gone from his eyes. He barely touched his peanut butter sandwiches. Jessie found herself talking nineteen to the dozen, just to cover up the silence round the table. In the end she ran out of things to say, so she asked Jack about the phone call.

'Is your dad sending them then, the gloves and things?' Jack nodded, but he didn't even look up.

At last her father spoke up. 'I tell you what, how would you two like to come fishing tomorrow? Bit too much of a swell for the boat. We'll try the rocks. There's mackerel about and bass. Have you ever done any fishing, Jack?'

'Some.'

'That's settled then. After school tomorrow. I'll pick you up.'

All through school the next day, Jack hardly spoke to anyone. In playtime, in spite of all Marion's begging and badgering, he left Marion and Liam and the Pirates to their training, and went to sit by himself on the wall. Jessie joined him.

'You all right?' Jessie asked.

'My Dad's sick, really sick,' Jack said quietly. 'He sounded really bad on the phone. He's going to have surgery. It's because I lost my arrowhead. I know it.'

'What's he got?' Jessie asked.

'Something's wrong with his heart. He said he needs a new valve.'

'That's nothing,' said Jessie. 'My gran had that, and she's fine now, honest.'

'You sure?' Jack said, the life in his voice again.

'Course I am.'

Just before the end of playtime, Marion Murphy came over to them, swinging her baseball bat. As usual she had her whole pack with her. 'You changed your mind yet, Jessie Parsons?' she demanded. Jessie shook her head. 'Well, we've all decided. We're not speaking to you till you do, not a word. None of us.'

Jack jumped down off the wall and put himself between them and Jessie. 'Why don't you guys get lost!' he shouted. No one had ever heard him like this before. 'Why don't you just leave her alone?' And he pushed through them and walked away. But Marion was as good as her word. No one spoke to Jessie. They'd just look at her and smile amongst themselves. It was the longest school day she'd ever lived through.

Her father met them in Clatterbang at the school gates and drove them across the island to Portlea. He was prattling on about the last bass he'd caught off the rocks at Portlea. 'Ten pounds it was, and not a word of a lie,' he said. He looked at them in the rearview mirror. 'Not the happiest pair I've ever seen,' he said. 'What's going on?'

'Nothing,' said Jessie.

'Well, you could have fooled me,' said her father. 'Whatever it is, the fishing will help. A great healer is fishing. You haven't quarrelled, have you?'

'No,' said Jessie firmly. But she said no more.

Her father was right about the fishing. There was the heart-stopping clamber down the rocks clutching her father's hand. There was the wind and spray on her face, and the great grey sea heaving in towards her. All her troubles were soon forgotten. And Jack was his old self again. Jessie's father fixed up a rod and line for him and helped him with his first cast. He didn't need any more help than that. Jessie watched him. Each cast was more expert than the one before. He knew what he was doing. Jessie always loved this place. She couldn't hold a rod, not to fish with; but she didn't mind. She was happy enough just watching them both, and listening to them wittering on about engines and turbos, pistons and filters and suchlike. And when she tired of that, there were the cormorants and shags to look at, standing like black sentinels on their rock below her, wings outspread and drying in the sun; and there were the gulls too, and the fulmars and the terns swooping and screaming overhead.

A mist was creeping in over the sea and Jessie wondered if there was any real difference between clouds and mist. She was already cold, and her legs ached, but she didn't mind. She was just thinking about Grania O'Malley again when she heard her father curse loudly.

'Lousy reel's jammed again,' he said. 'It's never been any good. And there's fish about too, I can smell them. Listen, can you two look after yourselves for a while? I'll just pop back home for my old one. Old-fashioned it may be, but at least it never lets me down, not like this beggar. You stay where you are, Jess, and you too, Jack, y'hear me? No climbing down. There's a wicked-looking swell out there today. Stay put. I shan't be long.' And he took his rod and was gone, up over the rocks to the cliff path. Jessie heard Clatterbang starting up.

'Hear that?' Jack called out. 'Starts better already. I'm a genius with engines, a real genius.'

'Any luck with the fish, genius?' she called back. Jack never answered. He just reeled in and cast again. In her armchair of rock, Jessie was too far away from him to talk properly. They had hardly said a word to each other since the incident in the playground. She wanted to talk. So she left her rock and sidled towards him on her bottom, until she was sitting right beside him and looking down into a cauldron of surging sea. 'I don't care, you know,' she said. 'I don't care if they never speak to me ever again. I don't care. They can stuff themselves.'

That was the moment the fish caught on and Jack shouted, 'I've got one! I've got one!' He braced his legs and began to reel in furiously. Then he slipped. His legs went from under him and he was sliding past her towards the edge.

Instinctively, Jessie reached out for him. For a fleeting moment she had hold of his jeans, just long enough for Jack to cling on to a rock and stop his slide. But then Jessie herself was slipping, rolling over and over and over, trying to find something to clutch at, anything. But there was nothing, no way she could stop herself. She caught a glimpse of Jack throwing himself full-stretch on the rock to save her. Then she was over the edge and falling through the air. The sea smothered her before she could scream. The water came into her mouth and into her ears and she was sinking deeper and deeper and could do nothing about it.

She looked up. There was light up above her, light she knew she had to reach if she was to live, but her legs wouldn't kick and her flailing arms seemed incapable of helping her. She had often thought about how drowning would be, when she was out in her father's boat or crossing over from the mainland on the ferry. And now she was drowning. This was how it was. Her eyes were stinging, so she closed them. She closed her mouth too, so she wouldn't swallow any more seawater. But she had to breathe – she couldn't help herself. She gasped and the seawater came in again and she began to choke.

Then something was holding her down. She fought, but the grip tightened about her waist and would not let go. Her head broke water, and suddenly there was air, wonderful air to breathe. She was spluttering and coughing. Someone was shouting at her. It was Jack and he was holding her. 'It's me! It's me! Hang on, just hang on to me. You'll be OK.' His face was near hers. 'Can you swim?' She shook her head. 'Just try to keep your mouth closed. Someone'll see us. We'll be OK. We'll be fine.'

Jessie looked beyond him. The shore was already a long way off and they were being carried away from it all the time. She looked the other way. Whenever they came up to the top of a wave she could see the bank of mist rolling over the sea towards them. One more wave and the mist would swallow them and then no one would ever see them.

'We've got to keep floating,' Jack cried. 'Just hang on.' The cold had numbed her legs already and she knew her arms couldn't hold on much longer. And then the mist came over their heads and shrouded them completely. Jack was crying out for help, screaming. She tried herself, but could only manage a whimper. It was hopeless.

From out of the mist came the unreal sound of oars dipping in rhythm, of men's muffled voices calling over the sea. Jack cried out again and the rowing stopped almost at once. They heard the sea slapping the sides of a boat, and then they saw it. It loomed out of the mist, riding the waves, its rearing prow ploughing through the sea towards them. There were arms pointing, heads leaning out, and then an oar to cling to. Rough hands reached for them, hauled them in over the side and they lay on the bottom of the boat gasping like landed fish. The faces that looked down at them were unshaven and weathered. One of them wore a black eyepatch. None of them was smiling.

7 ROCKFLEET

BY THE TIME THE MIST LEFT THEM, THEY WERE
out of the swell of the open ocean and in amongst the
sheltered islands of Clew Bay. The boat moved faster
through the water now, the men rowing more evenly, their
strokes longer, deeper. Jessie and Jack sat shivering side by
side, covered in a huge cloak of skins. There were fifteen
men rowing on each side, and the boat – which was more
like a great open galley – must have been longer than the
Clare Island ferry, thirty yards or more, with a pointed
prow and her raised stern covered in by a canvas roof.
There was a tall mast for a sail, but no sail was set. The men
at the oars cast hard, searching looks in their direction.
They had the least hospitable faces Jessie had ever seen.

'Who are they?' Jack whispered through chattering teeth. It was the first time either of them had dared talk.

'I don't know,' Jessie said. She thought for a moment of jumping overboard and escaping, but knew at once that she couldn't do it. She hadn't the strength even to stand up, let alone swim; and besides, she'd had quite enough of swimming for one day. Completely exhausted by now, Jessie drifted into sleep against Jack's shoulder.

She was woken suddenly by a splash and a barked command. She heard an anchor chain running out. They shipped the oars and the galley was gliding silently through still water before grinding to a halt in the shingle. Jessie looked up. Now she knew exactly where she was. Above the prow of the galley, stark against the sky stood a castle, Rockfleet Castle. It rose sheer from the rocks, a tall stone tower with ramparts round the top and slits for windows. She had often been past it in the car on her way to Gran's house on the mainland, and had stopped to look more than once; but the door had always been locked and they could never get in. She remembered her father pointing out the stone drain where the lavatory emptied out into the sea, and her mother saying it must have been a bit draughty, and her father laughing; but that was all she could remember about it.

The men were leaping out over the sides now and

splashing ashore through the shallows. They were dressed peculiarly, in long baggy breeches, in rough shirts that were too big for them, and most had some kind of jerkin made out of leather or canvas. All of them carried swords at their sides.

Jessie found herself picked up and dropped unceremoniously overboard into the arms of one of the sailors who grinned down at her toothily out of his gnarled face – the kind of man who slits throats, she thought. Then he was carrying her up the beach, over the rocks and in through the castle door. She was in a small low-ceilinged room. From the shadows all around, grizzled faces stared at them, eyes glowing in the dark. Many were bearded, and most wore woollen caps pulled down to their ears. And then came a voice from somewhere above them and it was a voice both of them recognised at once, the voice of Grania O'Malley. 'Will you bring them up here to the fire, boys, and fast. They'll die of the cold.'

Jack was ushered on ahead up the narrow, winding stone stairs. Jessie still had to cling tight to her sailor, leaning her head inwards to avoid bumping it against the walls. The stairs brought them out into another room about the same size, but lighter. Here the floor was covered in rushes and there were tables set for eating. But there was no one there. Then they were climbing more winding stairs until at last Jessie was set down on her feet in front of a great crackling fire. Jack was beside her. Her hand crept into his and gripped it. He squeezed back. It was some reassurance, some comfort. Again, there seemed at first to be no one else in the room. Then one of the shadows moved and became Grania O'Malley. The yellow of the flames lit her face as she came towards them. She was dangling something from her little finger, something that glittered and glowed, like gold. It *was* gold. It was the earring.

'I think you dropped this on the Big Hill, remember? Here, let me put it on for you, so's you won't forget it again.' Jessie's face was so cold that she could scarcely feel the fingers that touched her. 'Don't lose it now, will you?'

It was some time before Jessie could find her voice to speak. 'Are you really her?'

'If you mean, am I Grania O'Malley?' she said with a smile, 'then I am, indeed. Granuaille, Grany – they call me all sorts. The English call me Grace, but I'm always O'Malley even to them, and that's the bit that counts, isn't it, Jess? Your mother's an O'Malley, am I right? So, you and me, we're O'Malleys both. So's half the island, and you too, Jack.' She leaned towards them, hands on hips. 'It was my boys who fished you out of the sea and brought you home. Good boys all of them – well, maybe not good exactly – but fine pirates all the same, the best. We've been keeping an eye on you, so we have. If I couldn't be there myself, then I'd always have the boys looking out for you. Just as well too, wasn't it? Now come over by the fire, why don't you, and dry yourselves out. We'll fetch you some hot soup. You'd like that, wouldn't you?' Jessie hoped Jack wouldn't insist on a peanut butter sandwich and a Coke. He didn't.

What was in the soup neither of them knew nor cared. It was some kind of thick broth and it warmed them from the inside; and there was bread to wipe around the bowl when they had finished, coarse bread that you had to chew, full of grain and grit. But they didn't mind. Grania O'Malley smoked a pipe and studied them from her chair while they ate. Jessie could just about feel her hands again now, but she was still numb from the waist down.

'Should I rub your legs for you like your mother does?' Grania O'Malley asked. 'Would you like that?' How does she know about that? Jessie thought. And how does she always seem to know what I'm thinking, what I'm feeling? 'I told you, Jessie, we've been keeping a watchful eye on you. Call me your guardian pirate, if you will. I've been in school with you, I've met your Mrs Burke, your Miss

Jefferson too. I've been in church with you, with Father Gerald. I've been in your room – but I think you know that already, don't you? I was out in the sheep shed when you were shearing the sheep. And I was with you up on the Big Hill, wasn't I? You see, Jess, I've a debt to pay you. Pirate I may be, but I always pay my debts.'

'I don't understand,' said Jessie.

'Well, of course you wouldn't. Why should you? But what if I tell you that I was the skull you found? That's right. I am Smiley. You kept me and talked to me, remember? You told me your troubles. I got to know you inside out, Jess. And then, out of the kindness of your heart, you buried me back where I belonged. That was a fine and a good thing you did for me. It made me feel needed again; and whenever Grania O'Malley feels needed, she comes back, and where she goes, her boys go too. So we've come back for a while, not to haunt you, but maybe to help you out a little. That was the idea in the beginning anyway. But as it turns out, I think I'll be needing you as much as you'll be needing me. Now will I rub some life into your legs or won't I?'

She set aside her pipe and held her hands to the fire for a few moments. Then she knelt down beside Jessie, and began kneading, slapping and rubbing, until Jessie's legs began to tingle back to life. Grania O'Malley looked up at Jack and blew into her hands before she began again. 'See that chest over there, Jack? Have a look, why don't you?' Jack got up and walked across the room. He lifted the lid on the chest under the window. It was heavy and needed both hands.

'Gold!' he whispered. 'It's all gold!'

Grania O'Malley frowned. 'Not that chest. There's my whole life's winnings in there. Get out of it, out of it! I meant the other one, over there by the flag in the corner, the little one. Do you see that flag, Jack?'

Jack held it out to look. A red pig was striding across a black background under a small rearing horse, red too; and the whole thing was decorated with crossbows in each corner, and at the bottom was a ship just like the galley they had come in.

'I tell you, Jack, in its time that red pig put the fear of God into every sailor that set eyes on it,' said Grania O'Malley. Jack let the flag fall and was fumbling now with the lock on the smaller chest. 'That's the one,' she said. 'You'll find in there all the really precious things I ever had,' she said. 'I have a book of poems by Sir Philip Sidney, signed by the man himself. He turned a lovely phrase, and he was a lovely man too. It wasn't his fault he was an Englishman.' Jack had the chest open by now and was reaching in.

'Where d'you get this?' he said, and he was holding up in his two hands the shell of a strange prehistoric-looking brown crab with a tail like a sting-ray. 'That's a horseshoe crab,' Jack went on. 'We've got them back home, on the beach, thousands of them.'

'And that's just where I found it,' said Grania O'Malley. 'Course I couldn't swear it was from the same beach, but not so far from what you call Long Island these days. Oh, I know where you're from, Jack. I've been listening in, remember?'

'You've been to America?' said Jack.

'Isn't he the clever one now? And how else would I have such a thing? Of course I have. The boys and me, we all went there together. So we had a bit of luck. When all's said and done, life's nothing but a gamble. You need a bit of luck. We had a map, from a Portuguese privateer that needed teaching some manners. Well, the fellow was sneaking into Galway Harbour, and without so much as a by-your-leave. He should have paid his dues like everyone else. We weren't going to have it, were we? We took everything he had. He didn't have much; but he did have a map of the east coast of the Americas.' She turned to Jessie. 'Is your legs any better now?'

'A little,' said Jessie.

'Got to get you warm,' she said, flexing her fingers.

'You too, Jack. Come here, closer to the fire.' And she beckoned him over. 'You're an American, so I suppose you've got a right to know. I'm going to tell you something no one else in the living world knows, not even Mister Barney – and over the years I've told him plenty. Good fellow is Mister Barney, good company. But first we've got to get that chill out of you. Come closer, boy.' And she sat Jack down with his back to the flames. 'That's better.' And she started on Jessie's legs again, talking as she rubbed.

'There's not much I like about being a ghost, I can tell you, but at least I don't feel the cold any more like I used to. Five castles I had, and each as cold as the other. Worst of all was that draughty place on Clare down by the quay. Rockfleet was the best, but this too was a bitter cold place to live through the winters. Not like America, where the sun warmed you through to your bones. I tell you, it's a place I'd have stayed, given half a chance. We were there first too, before the Hollanders, and before the infernal English. You don't believe me, do you? Well, no one believed me then, not even my own miserable husband. But I was there, I tell you. I was there.'

She spoke low now, and in earnest. 'There was trouble at home, there was always trouble, but this time it wasn't something I could fight my way out of, or talk my way out of. The English were hounding me and the Scots were raiding down from the North, and my husband was nothing but trouble. I took the Portuguese map, I took my son and I left. We had one galley, thirty good boys and all the food and water we needed, and we went westwards, towards the setting sun. Three months at sea, hardly a drop of water left and the boys weren't at all happy with me. Then I got lucky. We sighted land. America.'

She pointed to the flag. 'That was the very same flag I took with me. I planted it at the top of the dunes. The place was a paradise. Fruit, fresh water, game, fish, all you wanted. How we lived! We were going to stay for ever. None of us wanted to come home. But then one morning, it all went wrong. My little boy, called Tibbott he was, went off along the beach looking for his crabs, just like that one. He had dozens of them already, but he had to have just one more, didn't he? He disappeared, vanished into thin air. We looked everywhere. Nothing. The next morning we woke up and there were Indians all around us – hundreds of them and they weren't at all friendly. They shot an arrow at me, missed me by a whisker. Landed in the sand right by my foot. And there was my little Tibbott, taken as hostage. The boys wanted to fight it out, but there's a time to fight and a time to talk. This was a time to talk. It was a simple deal. I could have my son back if we left and didn't come back. We none of us spoke the language of course, but we got the gist of it. They let us take all the food and water we needed, the flag and one crab shell for my son, and the arrow that nearly killed me. Not a lot to show for it. So there y'are. Now you know what no one else knows, that the Irish were first in America.'

She sat back and smiled at them. 'I *owned* America. It was mine and I lost it. And then I managed to lose it a second time, didn't I?'

'How?' Jessie asked, and by now she had quite forgotten that she was talking to a ghost.

'It was that son of mine, that Tibbott, the one who went collecting crabs in America. I deserved better. He was maybe twenty by now and wild in the head. He got himself shut up in prison by the English – well, that wasn't difficult, it happened to a lot of people. I spent a year or two behind bars myself, and it was no fun at all, I'm telling you. They'd have hanged him given half a chance, but I wasn't going to let that happen. A mother hen has to look after her chicks, doesn't she? So the boys and me, we sailed for England, up the Thames to Greenwich to see the English queen, Queen Elizabeth herself. I sent ahead and told her I was coming, that I wanted to see her. I was polite about it mind. Always best to be polite if you want to get what you want. I said to her, I said: "I want my son out of your jail. He's done nothing wrong." Which wasn't strictly true.

'And she says to me, she says: "What's in it for me?"

'And I replied quick as you like, "How would you like America?" So it wasn't mine to give, but she wasn't to know that. "It's mine," I told her, "It's Irish."

' "Indeed?" she said, all smiling and hoity-toity. Anyway, to cut a long story short, she took America for the English, and I had my son back – so I hadn't lost anything I hadn't lost already and I'd got what I wanted out of it. Happy as a lark I was. Only, as I was leaving, she says to me: "You're a bit of a pirate, aren't you?"

' "Sometimes," I replied.

' "So am I," she said. "But don't tell anyone. And listen, Grania O'Malley, if you're going to pirate from now on, then do it quietly so's no one notices, then we shan't have cause to disagree." I tell you, that queen was a woman after my own heart.'

She threw a log on to the fire and nudged it in with her bare foot. 'Well, there you have it, my life story in a crab shell. But that's all done with and a long time ago. These last centuries, the boys and me, well, we've been sort of waiting around. You don't like to interfere once you're dead, but there's times when you just can't sit by and watch. There's times when you're needed. And in recent years I've not liked what I've been seeing, what I've been hearing. Dead or not, these are my lands, my sea. All my life I defended them as best I could. Sometimes we won, sometimes we lost. And I never minded the losing, because I always knew we'd win in the end. Invasions and occupations, they come and they go – the Normans, the English, the Scots. They've all come and they've all gone. We've had the famine, we've had the plague. There was nothing a poor ghost could do but watch and weep. But the Big Hill on Clare, once they do that you can't put it right afterwards. There are some things time won't heal. I'm with your mother, Jess, and with you. One way or another, the thing has to be stopped.'

'But no one listens, do they, Jack?' said Jessie. 'Mum's told them and told them, but they don't listen. It's the gold. They're all greedy for the gold.'

'And you can hardly blame them, can you?' said Grania O'Malley. 'After all, they're only human, aren't they? It's a natural enough thing to be greedy – not good maybe, but natural. I was quite keen on the gold myself at one time. I never knew a pirate that wasn't. Now listen, me and the boys, we've been pondering this for some time now, and we've all agreed that the treasure in the big chest over there is not a lot of use to us any more. I mean, all we do is gamble with it, and we can do that with the pebbles from the beach just as well. I'll not pretend they're at all pleased with the idea of parting with it, but they know as well as I do, that it's in a good cause. And besides, they do what they're told – mostly.'

A gleam came into her eye. 'I've been waiting for just the right moment, and this is it. When you're all dried off again, the boys will row you home to Clare and drop you off, not that far from where they found you. There's a cave there – Piper's Hole, we used to call it. I've hidden in there a dozen times when the English came looking for me. It's maybe the deepest cave on the whole island and you can only get at it from the sea. It'll be just perfect. And guess what you'll find at the very back of the cave, undiscovered for close on four hundred years? The lost treasure of Grania O'Malley. Are you beginning to catch my drift?'

She got up and walked over to the chest under the window. She lifted the lid. 'This treasure came from the *Santa Felicia*, one of the great galleons of the Spanish Armada, driven on to the rocks in the worst gale I ever saw. We rescued most of the crew, and the treasure, and the captain too – Don Pedro. He was a sick man, so I nursed him like a good Christian woman should. He was handsome too, eyes so dark you could drown in them – but then that's another story.' She seemed suddenly sad. 'Another story for another day maybe. Let's just say that, ever since, we've been keeping Don Pedro's treasure for a rainy day, and now the rainy day has come. There's more gold in this chest than they'll ever find inside the Big Hill. It'll be you that finds it, so by rights it'll be you that decides what's to be done with it. All you have to do is to tell them that you're happy for everybody on the island to share the treasure, providing they leave the Big Hill alone. How would that be now?'

'That's cool,' said Jack, a broad grin on his face, 'that's real cool.'

'That's what I thought too,' said Grania O'Malley.

'Can I look?' Jessie asked. Her legs were stiff with cold, and walking wasn't easy, but she had to get up and look. The chest was filled to the very top with gold cups, gold plates, gold doubloons, and gold chains. There were crosses that sparkled with emeralds and rubies, there were rings and pearls and bracelets and necklaces, and heaven knows what else.

'Is this where my earring came from?' she asked.

'Both of them,' said Grania O'Malley.

Jessie dug her hand in, cupped a handful of coins and let them run out through her fingers. 'It'll work,' she said.

'It'll really work. Once they see this, once they touch it they'll forget all about the gold on the Big Hill, they're bound to.' They looked up together as they heard a helicopter flying low overhead. 'They'll be out searching for us,' said Jessie. 'My mum and dad, they'll be worried sick.'

'They won't have to be worried for much longer,' said Grania O'Malley. Jack ran to the window. The helicopter was heading out over the islands of Clew Bay, out towards Clare. 'We'll get you home soon enough,' said Grania O'Malley. 'We'll wait just a little for the high tide to float the galley off the beach and then we'll be on our way.' She was gone down the stairs and they were left alone.

Jack stared down into the chest. 'I do not believe this,' he said. 'I just do not believe this.' Jessie draped a necklace around his neck and filled his hands with coins.

'Believe it now?' she said.

There were raised voices downstairs, and then they heard Grania O'Malley shouting above the others. 'Will you be still and just listen! Did I ever let you down, did I?'

'Yes,' said one of the pirates.

'Well, maybe I did, but not often. And we always shared and shared alike, the good times and the bad? And we all agreed, didn't we? The treasure has to go, so we can save the Big Hill.' There were still rumblings of discontent. 'Tell me this, will you?' she went on. 'Being a rich ghost, does it make any one of us happier? Well, does it?' There was a long silence. 'Brendan, Donal, upstairs with you, and get that chest down. And be nice to those children while you're at it. Try smiling, for God's sake. It won't hurt. There's nothing I hate worse than a bunch of sulking pirates.'

The two pirates that came up the stairs shortly after did try to smile at them, but not very successfully. They looked longingly into the chest for a moment, before they closed the lid and carried it away downstairs. It wasn't long after that Grania O'Malley came for them, took them back down the winding stone stairs, and led them out of Rockfleet Castle and into the bright light of day. Both she and Jack took a hand each and helped Jessie down over the rocks towards the waiting galley.

High in the stern, with Grania O'Malley sitting on the treasure chest beside them, they went one last time through the plan to be sure they all understood, but it was difficult for Jack and Jessie to concentrate. There were two helicopters buzzing about overhead. The lifeboat was out looking, and the ferry too. It looked as if every boat on the island was at sea. As they came out into the open ocean, out of the shelter of Clew Bay, the ferry passed within hailing distance, the deck lined with searchers –

Michael Murphy was there, Father Gerald too, and Mrs O'Leary from the pub. Some of them had binoculars trained right on them. But none of them seemed to be able to see them at all. The galley raced on, dipping into the wash the ferry had left behind, the spray showering everyone on board.

'You'd think they'd look where they were going,' laughed Grania O'Malley, wiping her face. 'Now have you been hearing me, you two? They only have my treasure if they leave off the mining on the Big Hill. Are we clear? It'll work a treat, you see if it won't.'

As they neared the shore, Grania O'Malley took the tiller herself and navigated the galley in through the surging seas. She waited for the right wave, gave the word, and then they surfed the crest of it through a narrow opening in the reef and into the calmer waters of a hidden inlet. Half the pirates shipped their oars now and scrambled forward, leaping into the sea and wading waist-high towards the shore. Heaving on the ropes, they hauled the galley in. They unloaded the treasure chest first, and with the greatest care. Then came the children's turn to be handed over the side. They were carried – a lot less carefully, Jessie thought – out of the shallows, up the shingle, and dumped on the beach beside the chest.

'We'll be off then,' said Grania O'Malley, 'before we

all change our minds.' The crew looked their last at the chest, like dogs that have had their favourite bones taken away. Grania O'Malley bent down and patted the chest. 'Parting is such sweet sorrow,' she said wistfully, and then she smiled at them. 'Shakespeare. Now there's a fellow I'd like to have met. Maybe I will one day. But there's a lot of things I never did that I should have done, and many more things I did that I should not have done. Maybe that's why I'm doing this. Who knows?'

She ruffled Jack's hair; and then stood, hands on her hips, looking down at Jessie. 'Well, do I get a kiss, or don't I?' Jessie did not hesitate. She reached up, put her arms round Grania O'Malley's neck, kissed her on the cheek and hugged her. 'I'll know it if you need me,' said Grania O'Malley, 'and not a word to a soul about me and the boys. Promise? They'd not believe you anyway.'

She turned and strode out through the shallows towards the galley. The last they saw of her, she was standing on the prow of the galley, just as Jessie had seen her in her dream. She waved, and the galley simply vanished. They were left standing alone on the beach, the treasure chest beside them, the retreating surf hissing over the shingle.

* * *

The chest was unbelievably heavy. At first they wondered if they could shift it at all. But they knew they had to. They didn't want anyone to see it until the time was right, until they were ready. It had to be hidden. One heave at a time they dragged the chest up the beach and into the dark depths of the cave until they could drag it no further. They were still sitting on it, trying to get their breath back, when they heard voices from high above them on the clifftop. 'Shall we answer?' Jessie said.

But Jack had noticed something. 'Not with your earring on,' he said. Jessie clapped her hand to her ear. She had forgotten all about it. She took it off quickly, and slipped it into the pocket of her jeans.

'Ready,' she said.

'Let's go,' said Jack, and they walked out of the cave and began to shout. 'Down here! Down here!'

Even as they shouted, their voices were drowned by the sudden thunderous din of a helicopter overhead. It hovered for some moments over the cliffs, swooped out to sea, dipped and turned back towards them. There was a man leaning out and waving, and then he was being lowered towards them. The down-draught blew Jessie on to her bottom and she stayed sitting where she was on the wet pebbles as the man landed and ran over towards her. He crouched down beside them. 'Nothing more to worry about,' he said. 'You'll be fine now, just fine. Bit cold, are you?'

'A bit,' said Jack.

'We'll get you back soon enough,' said the man. 'Ladies first, eh? I'll be back for you in a minute.' He put his hand on Jack's shoulder. 'Just stay where you are. Won't be long.'

He snapped Jessie into the dangling harness and up they went, turning and swirling in the air together. Strong arms grabbed her and hauled her into the helicopter. She was strapped in at once and smothered in blankets. It seemed no time at all before Jack was beside her in the helicopter, and they were skimming low over the fields, over the quay, over the abbey ruins and the school; and there was the farm below them, and the house, and the 'creatures' in the garden. Jessie found Jack's hand, squeezed it hard and got a squeeze back in reply.

As they landed in the field, the sheep scattering in all directions, they saw Jessie's mother and father come running out of the house and Panda too, his hair flattened along his back, barking at the helicopter. Mole was scampering away in amongst the sheep as fast as his legs could carry him. The hugging seemed to go on for ever, two at a time, and then all four of them together. Jessie thought they'd never let go. The helicopter rotors slowed at last to a whine and then stopped. There was quiet again, except for Mole braying his indignation, and Panda still barking at this extraterrestrial invasion.

There was a hot bath, hot chocolate and peanut butter sandwiches, and all the time the questions. Jessie answered them – that's what they had both agreed. She kept as close to the truth as possible. She had slipped on the rocks and fallen into the sea. Jack had dived in after her and saved her. They were a long time in the sea, and so cold, and then they'd been swept into this inlet and had found shelter in a a cave. Jack had tried to climb the cliff but he couldn't, so they just waited there in a cave. She kept it simple, and if they asked more, she said she couldn't remember.

Dr Brady was helicoptered over from the mainland to examine them. He said they were remarkably well, considering the ordeal they had been through. There were more questions. They stuck to their story and everybody seemed to believe them. There were cups of tea for the helicopter crew in the kitchen; and then the entire island, it seemed, came visiting. Even Marion Murphy came – and that was the first time she'd ever set foot in Jessie's house – but of course she turned out to be a lot more interested in Jack than she was in Jessie.

There were more tears, more hugs, and still more

questions. Through it all, Jessie could think only of how she was going to tell her mother and father about the plan to save the Big Hill without mentioning Grania O'Malley. It wasn't going to be easy.

She waited until everyone had gone and caught Jack's eye across the sitting-room. The time had come. She was still wondering how she was going to make it sound at all convincing when her father helped her. 'I still can't think how you managed it, Jack,' he was saying. 'The current against you, tide against you. And how come no one spotted you sooner? I tell you, it's a miracle, a miracle.'

'We were inside the cave a long time,' said Jessie, seizing her moment. 'I expect that's why no one saw us. It's deep, like a long tunnel and we just went in to get out of the wind, didn't we, Jack?' Jack nodded, but he didn't say anything. He clearly wasn't going to be much help. 'And then Jack went off exploring. That's when he found it.' They were looking at her, expecting more. There was no stopping now. 'We thought we should tell you first, didn't we, Jack? I mean it's ours, because we found it, and we've decided what to do with it, haven't we?'

'With what?' said Jessie's mother, completely bewildered by now. 'What on earth are you talking about, Jess?'

And that was when, quite unexpectedly, Jack spoke

up. 'Treasure. Gold. I found a whole chest of it at the back of the cave. Jess says it's Grania O'Malley's treasure, whoever she is.'

Jessie's mother and father looked at each other for a moment. 'Let's get this straight, Jack,' said her father. 'You were in the cave and you found a chest full of gold, is that what you're trying to tell us?'

'Yes, sir,' Jack replied. 'Right at the back of the cave, like I said. Pretty dark in there too, but you could see just about enough.' Jessie did her best to keep her smile inside herself.

Her father laughed, a nervous laugh. 'Are you kidding, or what?' he said.

'I can prove it too,' said Jessie triumphantly, 'I brought some of it back.'

'You've got some of the treasure, some of the gold? You've got it here?'

'Upstairs. In my jeans pocket. I'll fetch it.'

She found all her clothes where she'd left them, in a heap on the bathroom floor. The earring fell out as she picked up the jeans. Barry panicked when her hand came into his bowl and circled manically until Jessie had retrieved the other earring from under the stones. 'Not yours, you know,' she whispered. They were still silent in the kitchen when she came downstairs again. She beamed at Jack and opened her hand. Her mother took them from her one by one, and held them up to the light.

'They're beautiful,' she whispered. 'Just beautiful.'

'I pinched them,' Jessie said. 'I pinched them from the treasure chest. There's a whole lot of stuff like this, chains and crosses and plates – all sorts. And it's all gold, isn't it, Jack?'

Jessie's father was on his feet. 'And it's still there?' he said. 'Still in Piper's Hole?' Jessie nodded. 'I'll have to take the boat, and I'll need a torch.'

'I'm coming too,' said her mother, putting on her coat. 'You two stay here, stay in the warm.'

When they were quite sure they had gone, the two of them looked at each other, smiled and then burst out laughing. They laughed until it hurt, out of joy, out of relief. Suddenly Jack stopped laughing and grabbed her arm.

'Jess, I just hope Grania O'Malley hasn't changed her mind and come back and taken it away. Some of those pirate guys weren't at all happy about giving it away, you know, and neither was she.'

'You can trust her,' said Jessie, and she was quite sure of it; but the longer they waited the less sure of it she became.

It was nearly two hours later, and dark outside, when they heard Panda barking and Clatterbang come rattling up the lane. They ran outside. Jessie's mother and father were struggling to carry the chest between them across the yard. Jack ran to help, while Jessie held the door back for them. They heaved it up on to the kitchen table. Her father leaned on the table, shaking his head.

'You were right,' said her mother breathlessly.

'Have you seen inside?' Jessie asked.

'It's the real thing,' said her father. 'It's real treasure. I can't believe it. I just cannot believe it.'

'And it's ours,' said Jessie. 'All ours!'

8 MISTER BARNEY

BY THE TIME THEY HAD FINISHED EMPTYING the chest, the kitchen was glowing with gold, the dresser festooned with gold chains, the shelves lined with gold goblets and gold beakers. From every knob and every cup hook dangled a jewelled necklace. The table-top was almost invisible, covered as it was with doubloons and crosses, and gold plates piled high with glittering jewels. And in the centre, in pride of place, stood a great golden ewer with a fish's mouth for a spout. They sat down and simply gazed around them. Jessie put her earrings on and looked down at herself in one of the golden plates. For a long time no one spoke a word.

'Will someone please pinch me?' said Jessie's father at

last. 'This afternoon I thought for certain you were both of you dead and drowned and gone for ever – and here you are sitting in front of me all alive again. And now all this.'

'The lost treasure of Grania O'Malley,' breathed Jessie's mother. 'You're right, Jess. It has to be. It's old Mister Barney's story come true.'

'What do you mean?' Jessie asked, trying not to sound too interested.

Her mother sat back in her chair, quite unable to take her eyes off the treasure. 'And we all thought the old man was cracked in the head, his mind all to pieces. But he wasn't at all, was he?'

'For goodness' sake, Cath,' said Jessie's father, 'Mister Barney's stories are just stories. There's not a word of truth in any of them, everyone knows that. You'll frighten her silly.'

But Jessie's mother went on: 'I was about your age, Jess, when it happened. Mister Barney was already old, but he'd still cut more peat in a day than any man on the island. Us kids, we'd go up to his place to help him stack it sometimes, and afterwards he'd give us a drink of water and we'd sit down and he'd tell us all sorts of tales. I've forgotten a lot of them, but not this one. He told us how one day he'd been up on the Big Hill and he'd met the ghost of Grania O'Malley. He said how she'd got talking about her pirating days and how she'd fallen in love with some Spanish captain or admiral – I can't remember. Anyway, this Spanish captain was blown round the top of Ireland in his galleon – part of the Spanish Armada and all that – and was wrecked on the rocks. Everyone on Clare wanted to kill the lot of them, him and his crew. But she wouldn't let them do it – it seems she'd taken a bit of a fancy to him. She said there was no need to go killing anyone when they could have all the treasure they liked anyway. More Christian that way, that's what she told Mister Barney. So she saved her Spanish captain and his crew, and kept the gold. Everyone was happy.'

'Oh, come on,' Jessie's father interrupted. 'You can't seriously believe all that stuff.'

Jessie's mother gave him a long and withering look. 'As I was saying,' she said, 'she looked after the treasure herself and the captain and his crew stayed for a while. He was ill and she nursed him back to life. She told Mister Barney that it was the only time in her whole life she ever met a man she could be truly happy with. But then there was some quarrel, and the captain – I think he was called Don . . . Don Pedro, that's it, Don Pedro – anyway, he was wounded, and on his deathbed he made her promise she would take his crew safely back to Spain. So she did, but she kept his treasure of course. She hid it away because she didn't want the marauding English to find it. And then later, when she was older, she still kept it hidden – keeping it for a rainy day, that's what she told Mister Barney.

'Of course, we none of us believed him, not really. We wanted to, mind. I remember a few of us went digging for treasure afterwards, but we never found anything, so we soon gave up. Old Mister Barney didn't though. You'd see him out there with his metal detector, and in all weathers too, looking for Grania O'Malley's lost treasure. The older we got, the more we laughed at him. He found bits and pieces, a coin or two, not much. But then his hips gave up on him, poor old fellow, and so now he can hardly get about at all.'

Jessie's father was about to interrupt again. But she wouldn't have it. 'I'm not saying he isn't strange, Jimmy. I'm not saying it isn't an unlikely story, but will you just look at all this treasure! The story fits. And it's no good just saying he's crazy in the head. You heard him the other night arguing to save the Big Hill. You've seen his place. Packed to the gunwales with history books, isn't it? He's no fool. He's no idiot. The man knows more about this island than anyone else alive. I tell you, he's a walking encyclopaedia.'

Jessie listened, spellbound. She thought that maybe this was the moment to tell the whole story as it had really happened, confess that they had lied about finding the treasure in the cave, that they too had met Grania O'Malley just as old Mister Barney had. But then she thought again. Hadn't Grania O'Malley herself made them promise not to say a word? Hadn't she said that no one would believe them anyway? She was right. They'd just say she was making it up; and besides, Jessie hardly believed it herself. It was all too utterly fantastical.

Her father was snorting. 'Baloney,' he said. 'All a lot of baloney. I thought it was baloney before and I still do. He's mad as a hatter – it's a known fact. There's some things that just aren't possible. Ghosts is one of them.'

'Is that so?' said Jessie's mother acidly. 'Will you look at the coins on the table. Spanish doubloons, aren't they? I've seen others just like them, and you have too. If they are Spanish, then like as not they're from an Armada ship. It's a known fact that at least one of the Armada galleons was wrecked off Clare Island. For God's sake, don't people come here every summer and go diving on the wreck? Hardly surprising they haven't found much, is it? It's all been hidden away in Piper's Hole, for hundreds of years. You remember there was that cannon dragged up last year in the fishing nets? That was off the Armada galleon, wasn't it? You can't deny it. And everyone knows too, who's got any knowledge of it, that Grania O'Malley ruled in these waters at the time of the Spanish Armada. Now tell me, who else could all this belong to, if not to her?'

They were arguing again, and Jessie wanted to stop it. 'It doesn't matter whose treasure it was, Mum,' she said. 'It's ours now, Jack's and mine, and we've already decided what we're going to do with it, haven't we, Jack?' Jack smiled at her, but a little anxiously. That was when Jessie lost her nerve. Panic gripped her and her mind seemed to stall. She just couldn't think straight. 'You tell them, Jack,' she said, in desperation.

For some moments Jack looked down at his hands and said nothing. 'Well,' he began, 'we were in the cave, Jess and me, and we were figuring out what we'd do with all this treasure – you know, how we'd spend it. I said I'd like an old Studebaker or a Bugatti, remember, Jess? And you said you'd rather have a pair of new legs, right?'

Jessie could not believe her ears. He was brilliant.

Jack went on: 'Just talk, just dreaming, that's all we were doing. See, we didn't reckon we were going to get out of there. The tide was coming up real fast, almost into the cave, and we had nowhere else to go. We thought we were going to drown. So we made ourselves a promise.'

'What sort of a promise?' asked Jessie's mother.

'Not a promise, I guess, more like a deal,' Jack said. 'That's it, more a kind of deal. We said that if we got out of there alive, then we'd give all the treasure away, we wouldn't keep it for ourselves. We'd share it with the islanders. It was Jess's idea. She said that if everyone on the island had a fair share – and it looked like there was more than enough treasure to go round – then they wouldn't need to cut the top off the Big Hill, because they'd have all the gold they ever wanted. It seemed like a great idea to me. So we both promised that's what we'd do if we survived, and we did survive.' He looked straight at Jessie's mother, cool as a cucumber. 'She thought you'd like that. Isn't that right, Jess?'

Jessie was dumbfounded. Jack was a better liar than she could ever be. Her mother was holding her hands out to her, her eyes full of tears. 'Come here, Jess,' she said. 'I want to cuddle you the biggest cuddle you've ever been cuddled.' Sat on her mother's lap, Jessie was happy enough to let herself be cuddled. 'Well,' said her mother, sniffing back the tears. 'What do you think of this daughter of ours, Jimmy? Isn't that the most wonderful idea you've ever heard of in all your life? And you can't argue with it, can you? It's true enough. Jess and Jack found it, all of it, so it's theirs by right. And if they found it, then they should decide what happens to it.'

But Jessie's father was not looking at all enthusiastic. Whenever he was worried, he always sat with his hands together as if he was saying his prayers, thumbs under his chin, fingertips touching the tip of his nose. 'I'm not sure,' he mumbled. 'I'm not sure at all.'

'Well, of course you're not,' Jessie's mother said, her voice rising at once. 'That's because like the rest of the idiots on this island, you've set your heart on that stupid, iniquitous gold mine.'

'That's not fair and it's not true,' Jessie's father replied.

'Well, what then?'

'Look, it's just that I think we all need to think about this. It's not that simple. I mean, for a start, just because you find something, it doesn't mean it's yours. There's laws about these things. And even if it is yours, to share it out fairly you'd have to sell it and divide the money. How else are you going to share it all out? I mean, we don't know how much these things are worth, do we? You'll need an expert in treasure trove. Who's to say what that ewer, for example, is worth compared to that necklace or that beaker?' No one answered him, not for some time.

'Old Mister Barney,' Jessie's mother said suddenly, her eyes lighting up. 'You remember when those divers found that cannon last year? It was Mister Barney they fetched down to the beach, wasn't it? He dated it for them, and he told them all about it. Well, we'll do the same thing. We'll get Mister Barney down here, have him look at it all and tell us how much each piece is worth. He'll tell us what's what.'

Jessie's father took his hands from his mouth and nodded slowly. 'You're putting an awful lot of faith in that old man. But all right, I'll go tomorrow and bring Mister Barney back here, if he'll come. I don't know if he will though. He doesn't come out much these days, only when he has to.'

'You'll tell him what we've got here, Jimmy,' Jessie's mother said. 'And I'm telling you, he'll come, lickety-split. No problem.'

At that moment, there was a loud and insistent knocking on the front door and Panda was barking his head off.

'Only me, Mrs Parsons!' It was Mrs Burke. Never had the kitchen been cleared so quickly. With Panda careering round their legs, they scoured the kitchen for the last necklace or plate or beaker, slammed the chest shut, dragged it into the pantry and closed the door. 'Is anyone at home?' Mrs Burke was knocking again, louder this time. Jack was wiggling his earlobe at her frantically. Jessie took a moment or two to realise she was still wearing her earrings. She snatched them off and slipped them into her dressing-gown pocket. They were ready for Mrs Burke.

By the time Jessie's mother brought her into the kitchen, they were all sitting round the table and Jack was dealing a pack of cards. Panda was whining at the door of the larder and scrabbling at it. Jessie hauled her away. 'Always at the food, he is,' she said, by way of explanation.

'Well,' Mrs Burke beamed about her, 'aren't we the famous ones! Helicopters, lifeboats, whatever next? I've been over on the mainland all day – head teachers' conference, you know – and I missed all the excitement. Everyone's talking about it. It was on the radio. I just had to come and see for myself how you were.' Jessie was outraged. How could she be so sickly sweet and concerned in front of her parents, and such an old dragon back at school?

'That was kind of you, Mrs Burke,' said Jessie's mother, her eyes darting everywhere, looking for any stray treasure. 'As you can see they're fine, aren't you, children? Jessie fell in and Jack pulled her out. Saved her life, so he did. And now he's teaching us blackjack, aren't you, Jack?' She giggled at that, but nervously.

Mrs Burke clapped her hands in delight. 'My, my, a

real hero,' she cried. And then, all at once, her face creased into a puzzled frown. She was pointing at the pantry door. Everyone turned and looked. A gold necklace was dangling from the handle, a long chain of delicate gold links interwoven with flowers of white enamel.

'What a lovely, lovely thing,' breathed Mrs Burke. 'Yours?' Jessie's mother nodded. 'Gold, is it?'

'Wouldn't that be nice now!' laughed Jessie's mother. 'Of course not. I got it in Galway, last time I was over. Just a bit of tinsel, but I like it.'

At that Mrs Burke seemed immediately to lose interest and turned to Jessie's father. 'Mind you,' she went on, 'there'll be those, I've no doubt, who will be wondering what the two of them were doing left all alone out on the rocks like that.' Ah, thought Jessie, that's more like the Mrs Burke I know and love. And she was delighted to see that both her father and mother were looking daggers at Mrs Burke.

Mrs Burke cleared her throat in the silence. 'Well, I just thought I'd call in,' she chimed. 'Will I be seeing the children at school tomorrow?'

'I expect so,' said Jessie's mother, hustling her to the door. 'If they've recovered well enough.'

They heard the door close. Jessie's mother came back

into the room, leaned back against the kitchen door and closed her eyes. 'I know I shouldn't say it, seeing as she's Jess's teacher and all, but sometimes I could really strangle that woman, Miss Tittletattle that she is.'

Jessie was running the white enamelled necklace through her fingers. She tried it round her neck. 'Do you think she knew?' she said.

Jessie's mother shook her head and laughed. 'Course not. She'll be in every shop in Galway looking for one just like it. Now take that gorgeous thing off before someone else walks in. Come on, Jimmy, we'd better hide this lot away, and quick. And you two can get yourselves to bed.'

Tired as she was, Jessie did not want the day to end. She took her earrings out of her dressing-gown pocket, put them on and sat in front of her mirror. She smiled at what she saw. She looked like a real woman for the first time, like her mother, like Grania O'Malley. The dramatic events of the day kept churning around in her mind, the fishing from the rocks, the tumble into the sea, the rescue, the pirates, Grania O'Malley, the treasure, the helicopter, the plan to save the Big Hill. It was as if she was inside some wild and wonderful dream. Yet at the same time, she knew for sure it was no dream, that in the room next door was the boy who really had saved her life.

He had saved her life! In all the excitement she had forgotten that. She had never even thanked him.

Jessie did not want to be heard. Walking quietly was never easy for her, so she crawled along the passage and tapped lightly on Jack's door. 'Jack?' she whispered. 'Are you still awake?'

'I guess so,' came the reply. She reached up and opened the door. The light was still on. He was sitting up in his bed, propped against his pillows. 'You can't sleep either?' he said, as she got to her feet. 'I was just thinking about that horseshoe crab shell she had,' he went on, 'that maybe all those years ago she landed right on my beach on Long Island, that maybe I've walked on the same sand she did. That'd be amazing, wouldn't it?' Jessie sat down on the end of the bed. 'I've got this teacher back home, Mrs Cody. She's really up on history, you know, Christopher Columbus, the Pilgrims, the Revolution, the Civil War, all that stuff. Soon as I get back, I'm going to tell her she's gotten it all wrong – everyone has. The first person to land in America – on Long Island, anyway – wasn't Dutch or British at all. She was Irish, an Irish pirate called Grania O'Malley. Mrs Cody'll be real excited – she's Irish herself. Real excited. But then, I guess maybe she won't believe me. She'll just think I'm nuts.'

'But we're not nuts, are we?' Jessie asked. 'It really did happen, all of it, didn't it?'

'Sure it did, Jess,' he said. 'Kind of makes you wonder. I mean, if all of this really happened, and it did, then almost anything can happen, right? Maybe when I get back home, Dad won't be sick any more, even without my lucky arrowhead. No use just hoping. I guess you've just got to believe.' Jessie didn't know what to say. 'You know something else, Jess?' he went on. 'You're really lucky. Your mom and dad, even when they get mad at each other, you know they're just saying what they have to say. They don't want to hurt each other.'

'You think so?' said Jessie.

He smiled broadly now. 'And we fooled them real good, didn't we?'

'I don't know about Dad,' said Jessie. 'I think he knows something's going on, but he doesn't know what. And even if we told him, he wouldn't believe us, would he? No one would.'

'What wouldn't I believe?' The door was open and her father came into the room. 'What are you two cooking up?' he said.

'Nothing,' said Jessie.

'You still got those earrings on? Off with them, you little pirate. They belong downstairs with the rest. You'll be going to school in them next.' Jessie wanted to protest, to tell him the earrings were really hers and not part of the treasure at all, but she knew there was no point, not unless she told her father everything. Too many lies had already been told for that. She took them off and dropped them reluctantly into his hand.

'Where are you going to hide the chest?' Jessie asked.

'You bury treasure, don't you?' her father said. 'Your mum's outside now. We're digging a hole behind the hen-house. It'll be safe enough there, don't you worry. Now, to bed with you.'

Jessie was back in her room and sitting on the edge of her bed before she remembered she still hadn't thanked Jack for saving her life. She would have to do it tomorrow.

It was a long night and she couldn't sleep a wink. Her body wanted to drift away, but her mind simply would not let it. She could see Grania O'Malley's face so clearly in her head that she felt quite sure she must be there with her in the room. And then there was still the cloud of doubt that hung over their plan to save the Big Hill. Her father was right, to share the treasure out fairly amongst everyone, it would have to be sold. But what if old Mister Barney said it wasn't worth that much anyway? And worse still, what if he said it wasn't theirs to sell? What if? What if? She said her prayers over and over again, something she hadn't done for a long time; and it was in the middle of one of her long begging prayers, for God to make everything turn out all right, that she finally went off to sleep.

In school the next day she could not stop herself from yawning. She yawned when Mrs Burke had the two of them up in front of the whole school and thanked God for their rescue. Everyone seemed to have forgotten about not speaking to her, even Marion Murphy. When all the children gathered round them at playtime and bombarded them with endless questions about their adventure, she still had to yawn. It was good to feel popular. She wasn't as popular as Jack, she knew that; but not a word was mentioned about the Big Hill. Everyone seemed to have forgotten all about that too.

Jessie basked in it all, but the yawns kept coming and there was nothing she could do about it. Even when the newspapers and the radio and television people turned up and asked what it had been like and told them both to smile into the camera, she still had to stifle a yawn. It should all have been so exciting, but somehow it just wasn't. All she enjoyed of the day was the secret she and Jack shared, the true story of what had really happened, the story that no one else in the world would ever know – except Grania O'Malley and her pirates.

Only on the way back home after school did she manage at last to talk to Jack alone. 'Mrs Burke said we'll be on telly tonight,' she said. But Jack did not look at all happy about it.

'What's the matter?' she asked.

'Nothing much, just something Liam said.'

'What?'

'The diggers. His dad told him. They'll be over here by the weekend. We haven't got much time.'

'I wonder if Mister Barney's been yet?' said Jessie.

When they got home, Jessie's mother was singing in the kitchen, and that was something Jessie hadn't heard for a long time. 'We're going to be on the telly,' Jessie told her.

'I know, Jess,' she said, hugging her tight and then taking off her coat. 'Everyone knows. It's all over the island. Front page in The Irish Times tomorrow. I've had the newspapers on the phone, photographers in and out all day.' She kissed them both. 'I could eat the two of you, so I could. I could eat you, I'm so proud of you,' she said.

'Mum,' Jessie had to tell her, 'have you heard about the diggers coming?'

'I heard,' she said, and then she went on, 'but we're

not finished yet. I was thinking, Jess. I've been thinking all day. There could be another way of doing this, a quicker way, and without selling the treasure at all. We could take the whole lot round to Michael Murphy, here and now, and make him an offer he couldn't refuse. We could buy the Big Hill off him. Then it would be your hill, our hill. We could stop the diggers in their tracks. One look and he'd jump at it, I know he would. Your father thinks it's all wishful thinking. He's wrong. I know he's wrong. What d'you think?'

'It could work,' cried Jessie, seeing the sense of it at once. 'It could really work.'

'Has Mister Barney come over?' Jack asked.

'In the sitting room,' she lowered her voice. 'He's been here for an hour or more.'

'Well, what does he say?' said Jessie.

'Nothing, not yet. He just looks at everything through his magnifying glass, mutters to himself and that's that. You go in. I'll bring the tea in a moment.'

Mister Barney was sitting in the big armchair by the fireside, the open treasure chest on the floor beside him. He looked up as the children came in. Jessie had not seen him this close for some time. He seemed all skin and bone, somehow lost inside his great dirty coat. It was difficult not to stare at the raised veins in his hands.

'Jessie, isn't it?' he said. 'Haven't I seen you going up and down the Big Hill like a yo-yo?' He beckoned Jack closer to him and held out his hand to be shaken. 'And you must be the American boy.' He was looking Jack up and down. 'What do they feed you on over there? You should put some weight on you. Like a giraffe, you are. It was you that found all this, was it, and in Piper's Hole?'

'Both of us, sir,' said Jack.

'It is real, Mister Barney, isn't it?' Jessie asked. 'Real gold? Real Spanish treasure?' Mister Barney leaned forward, picked out a doubloon from the chest and examined it through a magnifying glass. 'I'll tell you all you need to know soon enough, Jessie, soon enough. Won't be long. Patience now.' He rubbed his hands and blew in them. 'What's next, Jimmy?'

Jessie's father dipped into the chest and brought out a gold cross encrusted with dark green stones. He laid it carefully on the table in front of Mister Barney who picked it up with loving care and peered at it long and hard. He grunted and set it aside. 'Next,' he said.

So it went on all through tea, all of them sitting in expectant silence and watching old Mister Barney for any sign of excitement or disappointment. There was none. When the chest was empty at last, he sat back and wiped his eyes with his handkerchief. 'I could do with a little glass of water, Cath,' he whispered. Jessie's mother hurried to the kitchen and fetched him one. Old Mister Barney sipped it slowly. 'That's lovely,' he said. 'Well, you'll be wanting to know what I think, I suppose.' He sipped again, agonisingly slowly. 'What I think is what I know for a fact. Now, do you want to hear the glad news first, or the sad news?'

'Glad,' said Jessie at once.

Mister Barney smiled at her. 'The same sweet thing your mother was at your age.' He turned to Jessie's mother. 'Do you remember, Cath, all those stories I used to tell you when you were little? Do you remember I told you once about Grania O'Malley's treasure? Well, there's not a doubt about it. You're looking at it. All my life I've been looking for this. This is off the *Santa Felicia*, the great Armada galleon wrecked in a gale off Clare in 1588. She told me she'd hidden it, but she never said where and I never dared ask her. I told you I'd met up with her ghost, didn't I?'

He smiled gently at Jessie's mother. 'I bet you thought I was cuckoo, didn't you? Drunk maybe. Well, I don't blame you. But it wasn't the drink. I've never drunk a drop of anything that wasn't water. I'm telling you now that I met her ghost – that's a plain and simple fact. She was a friend to me when I needed one, a real friend. And d'you know what a real friend is? A listener. And she was quite a talker too. I'm telling you now that this is the treasure of Grania O'Malley herself.'

'But is it worth a lot of money?' Jessie asked. 'We need to know how much.' Mister Barney seemed reluctant to reply. Either that or he hadn't heard properly.

'Mister Barney,' said Jessie's father, annunciating each word carefully, 'you remember I told you. Jessie and Jack, they found it. It's theirs. They want to share this treasure amongst everyone on this island so that then no one will need to cut the top off the Big Hill for the gold. To do that we've got to sell it.'

'I hear you,' said Mister Barney, and he reached out and patted Jessie's hand. 'I understand. That's a fine and noble thought, Jessie; and I could tell you the date of every piece, weigh it, tell you the worth of it too. But it wouldn't do you any good, I'm afraid, not you, not me, nor the Big Hill up there. And believe me, there's nothing I want more than to save that hill. It's come too late, Jessie. Now, if you'd found all this a few months back, then we'd have a chance. But your mother tells me the bulldozers will be over any time now to start their digging.'

'What are you saying, Mister Barney?' Jessie's mother asked.

'What I'm saying, Cath,' Mister Barney went on, 'is the sad news. You can't share it out, like Jessie wanted. And you can't use it to buy the Big Hill off Mr Murphy either, like you wanted, even if he'd sell it. You see, it's the law of the land that's in your way. If you find treasure like this, any treasure, you have to tell the Garda. You have to tell the authorities. I've looked into this for myself and I know it's right. You have to tell them and then they tell Dublin, and someone from the government comes and takes it away. They don't let you keep stuff like this. It's too important. It doesn't matter who finds it, it belongs to the nation, to the people. As soon as they hear about all this, and they would – you couldn't hardly keep it a secret, could you now? – they'll be coming for it, to take it away. They might pay you some compensation later, but it would be too late for the Big Hill. So you see, it isn't yours to share out. You want to save the Big Hill, then I'm afraid you'll have to find another way to do it. You'll have to find yourself another miracle.'

9 THE DIGGERS ARE COMING

MISTER BARNEY STAYED LATE INTO THE evening, the treasure spread out all round him. In all that time he scarcely stopped talking. It was as if he was trying to make up for all the years of silent solitude in his shack on the Big Hill. He pored over the treasure like a man obsessed, obsessed not with greed but with sheer joy at the discovery of it all. Every piece was a marvel to him. Again and again he revelled in the fact that he had at last been proved right about the lost treasure of Grania O'Malley.

'I tell you,' he said, 'it's terrible hard to believe in yourself when no one else does. That's why I like to hide myself away up on the Big Hill, out of sight of their mocking eyes. I don't care to be laughed at. And do you know another thing? I remember meeting Grania O'Malley up on the Big Hill. Clear as day I remember it, but in these last years, I've become more muddled in my head, and I'd begun to wonder myself if it was just my own imaginings I was remembering, and that maybe she was nothing more than that.'

He ran his hands lovingly around the gold plate on his lap. 'Now I know for sure that I really did meet her, and that what she told me was the truth. I have the proof of it, don't I?' He waggled a crooked finger at the children. 'I spend my whole life, searching the island end to end for this treasure, and I find nothing but a few miserable bits and pieces. You two go fishing, and find it without even looking for it!'

He laughed as he shook his head. 'Life's a pig sometimes, but then I suppose you'll not be needing me to tell you that, will you? Take the Big Hill. It's not fair what they're going to do and it's not right. They'll be moving me out of my place just because I'm in the way of their infernal diggers. They're going to cut the top off the Big Hill. It'll happen for sure now, and there's nothing more can be done about it. Still, now I've seen this, now I've touched it, I suppose I can't complain.'

He looked up at them, his eyes full of sadness. 'I've

tried to tell them that it's not right, but no one listens. They're all too young. The whole world is too young. Maybe you have to be old before you understand that what happens tomorrow isn't what counts, it's what happens in a hundred years' time – there's an awful lot of tomorrows in a hundred years. But the trouble is you don't know that till you've lived them. I've lived them.'

Jessie tried to listen, but she was tired by now and she had other things to be thinking about. She sat on the carpet, her chin resting on her mother's knee. Every now and again she would catch Jack's eye, and she'd know he was wondering exactly what she was wondering. Is Grania O'Malley in the room with us? Has she heard what we've heard, that her plan to save the Big Hill isn't going to work? What will she do now? What will we do now?

'What'll you do now?' Mister Barney asked, echoing her thoughts.

'I'm not sure,' said Jessie's father. 'I think maybe we'd all better sleep on it. And I think we'd best not say anything to anyone for the moment, Mister Barney – about the treasure, I mean.'

'And who would I talk to now, all alone up there in my house?' Mister Barney replied. 'I can tell my chickens, can't I? I'll have to tell someone at home, I'll be bursting with it.'

'Chickens are fine,' said Jessie's mother.

As he left, Mister Barney put his arms round Jessie's mother and hugged her. 'I'm sorry, Cath, so sorry,' he said. 'Maybe there's still a way to stop them. There has to be.'

'I hope so,' Jessie's mother replied. But Jessie could hear in her voice that she no longer had any hope left inside her. Jessie felt just the same.

While her father took Mister Barney back home, the three of them loaded the treasure back into the chest. Jessie thought of rescuing her earrings, but there just wasn't the opportunity, not with her mother there. They used a wheelbarrow to carry the treasure chest across the yard, and then they lowered it again into its hole behind the chicken shed. It was as they were burying it that her mother suddenly burst into tears and ran indoors. Jessie thought about going after her, but decided she would want to be alone. It was a still night, the sky full of stars, and the moon was riding through the clouds on the Big Hill.

Without warning, Jack called out into the night: 'Grania O'Malley, you're up there somewhere, aren't you? We've got a problem down here. The treasure's no good. The diggers will be here by the weekend, and we can't share the treasure like you thought. Unless you come up with something, and something really good, we're going to lose the Big Hill. I guess you've been watching, so you know how bad things are. Are you going to help us, or what?' The sea breathed softly in the distance and the abbey owl screeched once. The chickens shifted on their perches in the shed. But there was no answer from Grania O'Malley.

'Please,' Jessie begged, looking up into the sky. 'Please help us.'

'Think she's really listening?' Jack asked.

'She'd better be,' said Jessie. 'She'd just better be.'

Later, they were all round the kitchen table in their night things, sipping hot chocolate, except Jack who had his Coke as usual. 'You know what we forgot?' said Jessie's father. 'I just remembered. You were going to be on the telly, weren't you? I wonder if it's too late.'

He reached over and switched on the television. An advertisement was showing. Dozens of huge yellow diggers were working in a dusty quarry. A siren sounded and they all backed away from the quarry face, except for one. The driver was biting into a chocolate bar. He didn't seem to have heard the siren – either that, or he didn't care about it. There was a huge explosion above him. He wasn't bothered, he just went on with his chewing. The avalanche of rocks tumbled down towards him, and then suddenly froze in mid-air. He looked up, smiled, backed away in his own time, chewing and smiling smugly. Once he was out of the way, the avalanche thundered down, only just missing him. No one dared look at Jessie's mother. Then it was the local news. A smiling, simpering face came on.

'Good evening. Drama yesterday on Clare Island. Helicopters were called in, and the Westport lifeboat was launched when two children went missing. Ten-year-old Jessie Parsons, who suffers from cerebral palsy, was fishing off the rocks with her cousin . . .' And the report rambled on over aerial longshots of Clare Island. '. . . both are fit and well after their ordeal. So, everyone's smiling on Clare Island tonight.'

And there they were on television, the two of them, outside the school, Jessie lurching along beside Jack. Jessie got up and switched it off herself. 'Well, I'm *not* happy,' she stormed. 'And do they have to tell everyone about my lousy palsy? Do they?'

Upstairs she threw herself on the bed and hit the pillows again and again until the tears finally stopped. She felt the bed sag beside her, and then a warm tongue was licking her ear. Panda was panting in her face, tongue lolling and dripping.

It wasn't too long before her mother came up, as Jessie had hoped she would. 'You and me,' she said, 'we're a couple of old misery guts, aren't we?' And Jessie couldn't disagree. 'Still,' her mother went on, 'tomorrow can only be better, eh?'

But tomorrow wasn't any better. After morning prayers. Mrs Burke played the video tape of the television news bulletin in front of the whole school. Jessie didn't look. She tried to bear it as best she could, as everyone pointed at the screen, shrieking with delight when they recognised anyone or anything. Jessie spent most of that day looking out of the classroom window. She hoped, and she believed, that Grania O'Malley would appear from nowhere, that same smile on her face, the smile that would tell Jessie everything would turn out fine after all, that somehow another way had been found to save the Big Hill. But hope and belief often gave way to doubt, and doubt to despair.

At afternoon playtime she wandered away from the others, away from Jack who was still surrounded by infants clamouring for their hero's autograph. She found herself a hidden corner round the back by the kitchens, where she sat and waited on a dustbin for Grania O'Malley to come to her, or speak to her, anything. When she didn't come and she didn't come, Jessie began calling for her, softly, so that her voice wouldn't carry to the playground. She was still sitting on the dustbin and still calling for her, when she turned round and saw Marion Murphy staring at her.

'Who are you talking to?' Marion demanded.

'No one.'

'You were.'

'I was not.' Now there were more of them, half a dozen more.

'Well, anyway,' Marion's lip was curling ominously, and Jessie knew there was worse to come. 'You know where we're going? We're all going down to the quay after school. You coming?'

'What for?'

'The diggers are coming in, that's what for. You were going to lie down in front of them, remember?' They were closing in all around her. There was no way out. There was nowhere to run to. 'Well?' Marion said, thrusting her face into hers. 'Well?'

Jessie stared back at her and hoped they wouldn't notice the tears welling into her eyes. Suddenly Marion staggered backwards and fell, taking all the others with her, all together, like ninepins.

'You pushed me!' Marion screamed at her. 'She pushed me. The little cow pushed me!' Jessie sat on her dustbin and laughed out loud. She could not help herself. It was the sight of them all sprawled on the ground, their mouths gaping in astonishment. It was quite wonderful. Of course she knew at once who had done the pushing, and that meant she was there. Grania O'Malley was there, her or one of her pirates, it didn't matter. Either way, she knew without a shadow of a doubt that they had heard her. They knew what had happened about the treasure. And if they knew that, then they knew the diggers were coming. Somehow they would stop them, somehow they could still save the Big Hill. Jack was there now, Liam beside him. Marion was clutching her elbow and crying, still accusing. She was appealing to Jack. 'She pushed me! She pushed me! I'm telling Mrs Burke.'

'She pushed all of you?' Jack asked. Jessie was smiling at him from her dustbin, and he understood from her smile just what had happened.

Marion was scrambling to her feet now. 'That's it. You've asked for it, Jessie Parsons. You've done it now. If the diggers don't flatten you, then I will. You've asked for it!' And when she ran off, the others followed, promising as they went all manner of dire and terrible retribution. But Jessie didn't mind any more. Jessie knew now that Grania O'Malley was there, that no matter what, she would protect her. There was nothing to be afraid of. Liam and his friends were still gawping at her in disbelief when the school bell rang. She smiled at them.

'Bell's going,' she said nonchalantly, and she slipped down off her dustbin and tottered past them. 'Better not be late.' She felt so good, so triumphant.

When they got home after school, Jessie's mother wasn't there. There was no sign of anyone. Even Panda was missing. They were looking for the peanut butter to make up their sandwiches when they heard Clatterbang coming up the track, Panda chasing alongside, yapping at the tyres. Jessie went to the door. 'Where's the peanut butter?' she called out. Her mother and father had been talking to each other earnestly over the top of the car. Now they stopped, both of them looking at her. There was bad news. Jessie could see that much – and she could also see neither of them wanted to break it to her.

'We've just been up to see Mister Barney,' said Jessie's father.

'What's the matter with him?' Jessie asked. Jack was there too now.

'Nothing. He's fine.' Her father slammed the door and came walking round the front of Clatterbang towards them. 'He's fine, but he was the only one who could have known about the treasure – besides the four of us, that is. And even then, he couldn't have known where we'd hidden it.' The children looked from one to the other.

149

'It's gone,' said Jessie's mother. 'The treasure's gone.'

Jack ran across the yard towards the chicken shed, and Jessie followed as fast as she could. She found him staring down into an empty hole. 'I just can't understand it,' her mother was saying. 'I thought maybe one of us might possibly have mentioned to Mister Barney where we were hiding it, but we didn't. He didn't know anything about it. But we had to ask, just to be sure.'

'I told you, Cath,' said Jessie's father. 'Someone must have seen you burying it last night.'

'But it was dark, you know it was.' Jessie's mother was near to tears. 'Why do you keep trying to blame it on me?' The two children said nothing. They knew very well who had taken it.

'I didn't mean it like that,' Jessie's father said. 'But it has gone, hasn't it? That means someone's stolen it, someone on this island. It wasn't us, was it? And it certainly wasn't old Mister Barney. I told you there was no point in going up there. How could he possibly have moved a thing like that all by himself? There's only one answer. Someone must have seen us fetching it back in the boat from Piper's Hole. They must have spied on us, and then later on, watched us bury it. But who? Who?'

Jessie tried not to look across at Jack, but she could not

stop herself. It was the barest flicker of a smile, but her father noticed it. 'You don't seem very upset, Jess,' her father said.

Jessie shrugged her shoulders. 'Of course I am, but what can we do? If it's gone, it's gone. And besides it's no use to us any more, is it? Jack and me, we only wanted it so's we could share it out and save the Big Hill.' She turned to her mother. 'The diggers have come, Mum. Marion Murphy said.'

'I know,' said her mother quietly. 'I know.'

'There's four of them,' said Jessie's father. 'Down by the quay. They start work Monday.'

Jessie's mother walked away towards the house, talking as she went. 'You know, I'm beginning to wonder about all this. I'm really beginning to wonder. When we were kids, and Mister Barney told us he'd seen Grania O'Malley's ghost, we never believed him. When he said she'd hidden her treasure on the island, we never believed him. He spent his life looking for it, and we laughed at him. Then Grania O'Malley's treasure turns up, out of the blue.'

'So?' Jessie's father said, following her into the kitchen.

'You still don't see it, do you? If he was telling the truth about the treasure, and it seems he was, then it follows he was telling the truth about the ghost. And today, when we find the treasure's been dug up and taken away, what did he tell us? Grania O'Malley's come back for it, he says, because she knows it's no use to us any more. Well, if that's true, and let's just pretend it might be true, then it fits, don't you see. The whole thing fits. The children were *meant* somehow to find the treasure, and the treasure was *meant* to save the Big Hill. It was all her idea. Do you understand what I'm telling you, Jimmy? And now she knows it can't be done, because she's heard all about how it's not ours to share, how you can't just give treasure away when you find it. So she came to take it back.'

They were in the kitchen now, and she turned to face Jessie's father. 'I know it sounds mad, I know it does. But that's the gist of what Mister Barney said, isn't it? Well, I don't laugh at old Mister Barney, not any more. And there's something else you haven't thought of. No one has thieved anything on this island in my lifetime – maybe the odd sheep does go missing from time to time, but that's all. We leave the doors unlocked, don't we? The keys in the car, don't we? Does anything ever get taken? Think about it. I didn't dig that treasure up. You didn't, the children didn't, Panda didn't. If Mister Barney says it was the ghost of Grania O'Malley that dug it up, then you know what? I believe him. And if that makes me cracked in the head, then maybe I am.' And with that, she opened the drawer and took out the bread knife. 'I'll make you your sandwiches, Jack. And, Jess, why don't you help your father fill in that hole before a chicken breaks a leg?'

It was a weekend when time itself seemed to stand still. There was a calm and a quiet over the island, only a breath of wind off the sea. Even the owl in the abbey stopped calling at night. They dipped the sheep on Saturday morning, and through it all, Jessie's mother never said a word. She scarcely looked up. After it was over, Jack said he was off down to the quay. He wanted to see the diggers for himself, he said, and besides, the quay was on the way to the field and he was expected for a game of baseball with Liam and Marion and the others. It would be too far for Jessie to walk, if they had to hurry. 'Then you can push me in the wheelbarrow,' said Jessie. She did not like the idea of being left behind one little bit. Jack didn't argue. He laid some straw in the bottom of the squeaky wheelbarrow, and off they went, Mole and Panda tagging along behind.

When they reached the quay, there was a great crowd standing round the diggers. Everyone seemed to be there: Father Gerald, Mrs Burke, Miss Jefferson, Michael

Murphy, and dozens of others that Jessie had never seen before. The pub was overflowing into the street with people. Jack and Jessie left the wheelbarrow, made their way through the crowd and gazed up in awe at the gigantic bulk of the machines. Just the tyres were as high as Jack could reach. Painted on each of their yellow sides was one word, in huge black letters: 'Earthbuster'. Jessie saw them suddenly as living creatures, as monsters sleeping in the sun, but only for the moment. Once woken, they would rampage across her island and swallow up the Big Hill.

Marion Murphy was being lifted up on to a digger by a man in orange overalls. There were a dozen others dressed the same. Jessie soon worked out these must be the digger drivers, or maybe they were mechanics. They were swigging pints and rolling cigarettes as they folled up against their diggers. Swaggerers, Jessie thought, swaggerers every one of them. But the islanders were swarming around them and around their machines in open admiration. Marion had clambered on to the top of the digger by now, and stood there posing triumphantly, arms upraised, while her father took photo after photo of her. Jessie stared stonily up at her until she caught her eye. I'd give a lot, an awful lot, Jessie thought, for Grania O'Malley to push her off that digger. 'I hate you, Marion

Murphy.' Jessie tried to say it with her eyes, and must have succeeded because Marion looked away at once and posed again, more nervously now, an uneasy smile on her face.

'Let's go, Jack,' said Jessie. 'I've had enough.' But Jack wasn't there. She went looking for him, and found him at last round the front of a digger with one of the orange-overalled drivers who appeared to be showing Jack over the engine. She tugged at his coat, but he didn't seem to grasp how impatient she was to leave, nor how annoyed she was becoming.

'You see this, Jess? This guy says it's got to be about the biggest earthmover in the world. This is some powerful machine. Makes my Volkswagen at home look like a tricycle. How many horsepower, d'you say, sir?'

'Over five hundred,' said the driver, wiping his hands on an oily rag. He had ginger hair, Jessie noticed, a ginger that almost matched the colour of his overalls. 'Four-wheel drive, fuel injection. Thirty tons of power. Do anything you want, this will. Move mountains if you want it to.' He heaved with laughter at that, and then Jack was laughing with him and asking more questions about the engine. Jessie had had enough. She glared at them both and walked off.

Later, with Jack pushing her in the wheelbarrow along the road towards the field, Jessie was still bridling at what she saw as Jack's betrayal. He had been fraternising with the enemy, and she was furious with him. It was a long and silent walk. 'Something on your mind?' Jack said at last.

Jessie let fly. 'Don't you ever think of anything but engines?'

'Hey, I was just talking to the guy. What are you so mad at me for?'

'If you don't know, then I'm not saying.' And they relapsed into a simmering silence that lasted until they reached the field.

Liam and the others were already practising. As usual, Liam and Jack were the captains and they picked the teams; and as usual Marion managed to get herself picked for Jack's team. Jessie went off on her own and sat down under the tree. It was the first real argument she'd had with Jack, but it was entirely his fault and she wasn't going to make it up, not ever. She could see too, that he was really angry. He was winding himself up and pitching with real venom. No one stood a chance. They ducked and dodged and protested, but Jack just kept pitching. They hardly managed to hit a ball at all. And when it came to his turn with the bat, he belted the ball right over the fence and into the potato field beyond. He ran six home runs before they found the ball; and when they told him that wasn't fair, he said that he knew the rules better than they did.

Even after the game was over, she could see he was still furious. 'You coming or what?' he snapped at her. All the way home in the wheelbarrow she sat with her back to him, arms folded, lips pursed.

The evening was worse still. After supper, her mother sat staring into space. Jessie went and sat on her lap to console her and to be consoled. Jack phoned home, and then just took himself off to bed without even saying goodnight to anyone.

'Is something the matter with Jack?' her father asked.

'He's just sulking,' Jessie said.

'*He's* sulking!' Her father smiled wryly.

'Only one more day before they start.' Her mother spoke as if she were speaking to herself. 'One more day for the Big Hill.' And she looked up at Jessie's father. 'You know, somehow I always thought something would happen to stop it. First, I thought I could do it by talking to people, explaining, persuading. I couldn't. Then I thought that the people in Dublin must have more sense. They didn't. But even then, I still had faith. I don't know why, but I still believed it could be stopped. Then when the children brought us the treasure, I thought for sure that we'd win, that the Big Hill was reprieved. Just another false hope. And now I cling to anything, even

Mister Barney's ghost. I know it's silly, Jimmy, I know it's nonsense. But there's nothing else left, except prayer maybe. Am I going to pray in Mass tomorrow! I'm going to pray like I've never prayed before.'

'I'll pray with you,' said Jessie's father.

'You don't come to Mass,' she replied tartly.

'I can still pray, can't I?' he said. 'And I've a lot more faith in prayers than I have in ghosts, that's for sure.' He went on, 'Everywhere I went today, I kept looking at people, and thinking: was it you? Was it you that stole the treasure? Even Father Gerald, honestly. I'm telling you, one of them must have stolen it.'

Jessie lay in her bed that night and listened to Jack snoring in the next room. Every snore she heard made her angrier still. She made up her mind that she wouldn't speak to him the whole of the rest of his time on the island. Hadn't he laughed with that digger driver, and about the digger being able to move mountains too? He'd laughed! She felt so angry, and so lonely at the same time.

She longed to climb into her parents' bed and snuggle up to them and tell them the whole story of Grania O'Malley. She would tell her mother there and then not to worry, that Grania O'Malley would never stand by and watch the diggers move in on the Big Hill. But she just couldn't bring herself to do it. Even if her mother believed her – and maybe she would now – her father most certainly would not. And what if she did tell her story, and then Grania O'Malley didn't come back and save the Big Hill. What then? Where would that leave her? No, better to wait and see how things turned out.

The snoring stopped next door. She heard Jack's bed creaking, his door opening, and then footsteps coming along the passage outside her door. 'Jess?' He was whispering through the door. Pride would not let her answer. She pretended she hadn't heard. 'Jess?' The tiptoeing steps moved along the passage and then there was silence.

She wished at once that she had answered, but it was too late. Through her window she saw the full moon sitting on top of the Big Hill, too bright to look at, and anyway, she thought, you mustn't look at the full moon through glass. It makes you mad. She closed her eyes.

'Oh talk to me, Grania O'Malley, please,' she whispered. 'Please, please. Just let me know you're there.' Barry surfaced and splashed in his bowl. She said her proper prayers, closing her eyes tight shut. 'You've got to stop them, God. You've got to save the Big Hill. Please.' And she went on praying, until sleep overcame her.

* * *

Jack wasn't there when Jessie came down late for breakfast the next morning. Her father said he had gone off to play baseball with Liam. Jessie sat through Mass but could not concentrate. Either she was still fuming inside about Jack's treachery or she was watching the swallow high up in the roof, swooping down over the heads of the congregation and up to the rafters by the door, searching for a way out but never finding it. Her mother's knuckles were white under her forehead as she prayed. Jessie prayed to Jesus and to Grania O'Malley at the same time. She felt a little guilty about doing that in church, but she thought that Jesus wouldn't mind, that he'd forgive her just this once. As Father Gerald had so often said: 'Jesus understands, Jesus forgives. All you have to do is ask.' So she asked for forgiveness, and went on praying to both of them.

They were all standing and chatting outside the church door after Mass when Liam came racing down the hill on his bike, scooted to a stop, threw it down and came running up the church path waving his arms and shouting, 'It's sabotage! Sabotage! Someone's fixed the diggers.'

Father Gerald took him by the shoulders and calmed him down. 'What are you saying Liam? What do you mean?'

'Someone's fixed them. They won't work, Father. They won't start. None of them will.' Jessie and her mother looked at each other, a sudden bright hope in their eyes. Jessie felt a cheer of joy bursting to get out, but she held it inside her until she was alone with her mother in Clatterbang, and rattling along the road towards the quay, in convoy with everyone else.

'It's the ghost!' cried her mother. 'It's the ghost of Grania O'Malley, like Mister Barney told us. It's Grania O'Malley.' And the tears were running down her cheeks. 'Well, don't look at me like that, Jess. It *has* to be her, it *has* to be.'

'I know, Mum!' Jessie laughed above the clatter. 'I know!' And Clatterbang coughed loudly and backfired.

Jack was there with everyone else on the quayside. The digger drivers in orange overalls were gathered in a huddle and talking to the Garda. There was a Garda boat moored out in the harbour. People were still coming from all over the island, in Land-Rovers, on motorbikes, on foot. Mrs O'Leary was standing in the road outside her pub, still in her fluffy slippers. Father Gerald hadn't even taken his surplice off and it was flapping about him in the breeze. The whole place was a buzz of excitement. It was Mrs O'Leary who came over towards them as they got out of Clatterbang. 'Someone's fixed them, Cath,' she said. 'They don't know what's the matter with them. They just won't work, not any of them.'

'Well, it wasn't me, if that's what you're thinking,' said Jessie's mother, laughing. 'I wish it was, but it wasn't. But I think there'll be a few here who'll think it was.' And it was true. Several people were glaring at them, Michael Murphy amongst them. They walked away from Mrs O'Leary over towards Jack. 'If I told them who it really was,' Jessie's mother whispered to her, 'they'd not believe me, not in a million years.'

Jack had seen them now. He was sauntering over to join them, hands deep in his jeans pockets, baseball bat tucked under his arm. 'Hi,' he said, and he was grinning happily at Jessie. 'Never seen anyone half as mad as those digger guys,' he said. 'I'm going home. You coming, Jess?'

Jessie walked alongside him for some way, until they had left the houses well behind them, until she was quite sure no one could overhear them. Then she tugged at his arm and stopped him. 'It was *her*, wasn't it? She came!'

'Maybe, maybe not,' said Jack cryptically, and he wandered on. She tottered after him, dragging him to a stop again.

'What do you mean?'

He was laughing now. 'It wasn't my idea,' he said. 'It was your dad's. He doesn't believe in ghosts, not like us. He came to me and he said, did I know how to gum up the digger engines? I told him I could, anyone could, but first you got to find out a few things. So I went and asked that digger guy to show me his engine. You were there, right? Found out all I needed to know. Then, last night, your dad and me went and did it. I tried to wake you, but you were asleep. All you have to do is take off the distributor heads, and then pour a whole lot of sugar in the gas tank, and presto, nothing works. Told you, when it comes to engines and stuff, I can fix – or gum up – just about anything.'

'You did it?'

'I told you, me and your pa.'

'So it wasn't the ghost. It wasn't Grania O'Malley.'

'I guess not,' said Jack, and then, 'are we friends again?'

'I could hug you,' Jessie said. 'I could really hug you.'

'OK by me,' he said. And so she did. She felt like skipping all the way home, but she couldn't. She laughed instead, prattling on and on about how it served them right, about how she couldn't wait to tell her mother what had really happened. Jack said very little until they were nearly home. Mole came trotting down the road to meet them. Jack ran his hand along his back as he walked along beside him.

'It won't stop them, Jess, you know that,' he said, trying to break it to her as gently as he could.

'What do you mean?'

'Well, it'll maybe stop them for a day or two, but they'll soon fix it again. They've got to take them all apart and clean out the sugar – blocks the fuel injection. But once they clean them out, they can start them up again. We haven't won the battle or anything, Jess. We just put it off for a while, that's all.'

10 THE LAST STAND

THE DIGGER ENGINES HAD TO BE STRIPPED down, cleaned and reassembled. Jack went down to the quay after school each day to watch the mechanics at work. There were rumours, he said with a wicked smile on his face, that some 'bits' had mysteriously gone missing. But in the end, as Jack had predicted, their jubilation was to be short-lived. The missing parts were being helicoptered in from the mainland. The diggers would soon be on the move again.

The children were in school on the Wednesday morning when it happened and, much to Mrs Burke's annoyance, they all ran to the windows to look as the helicopter flew low overhead. That was just before lunch.

She was still trying to settle them down to work after afternoon playtime when some of the children began to hear a rumbling, like distant thunder. For some time Mrs Burke managed to keep them at their desks. But when Father Gerald was seen hurrying along the school lane, then everyone was at the windows again, necks craning, and there was nothing more she could do about it. The diggers were on their way. They could see them now. The roar of the engines was rattling the windows, and the classroom itself seemed to be throbbing and pulsating, so much so that Jessie had to clap her hands over her ears to stop them hurting.

She was the only one who stayed behind in her place. She did not need to see. She did not want to see. She looked up out of the window at the Big Hill, and through the mist of her tears she thought she saw someone standing there, right at the very top. She went over to the window. The figure was still there, and beckoning her. She knew at once who it was, and she knew at once what she had to do. She blinked her eyes to rid them of the tears, to see better. When she looked again, there was no one up there.

By this time, every child was fighting for a place at the playground fence. Mrs Burke couldn't stop them, and Miss Jefferson didn't want to - she was too excited herself.

It was Liam who opened the gate, and then they were all running down past the abbey ruins towards the road. There they were, all four giant Earthbusters trundling towards them along the coast road, a yellow convoy, billowing black smoke, orange lights flashing; and behind them a long line of Land-Rovers and pick-ups. In the fields on either side, the sheep scattered in terror, blundering into each other in their panic.

The children just stood and gaped, flailing at the pungent exhaust smoke and turning away to cough. Then Marion Murphy began to wave and cheer, and very soon they were all at it, all except Jack who had noticed by now that Jessie was not there. He went back inside the school to look for her and found her still standing by the window, still gazing out. She turned as she felt him behind her.

'It's what Mum always said,' she said. 'Ever since this thing with the Big Hill began, she's always said it. You want something badly enough, then you've got to do it yourself. No use waiting for someone else to do it for you. You believe in something, then sometimes you've got to fight for your beliefs, you've got to fight for what you care about, like Grania O'Malley did, like you did when you fixed their diggers. Well, now it's my turn.'

'What do you mean?' Jack asked.

'I thought Grania O'Malley would do it for us, but I was wrong. Maybe she's done all she could, maybe now she wants us to help ourselves. So that's what I'm going to do, help myself.'

She fetched her coat and bag from her hook and then called to him across the classroom. 'You coming?'

'You can't just cut school.'

Jessie looked around her and shrugged her shoulders. 'Well, everyone else has,' she said. 'Come on. We've got to hurry. We'll go across the fields. We can still get there before they do.'

Jack helped her through the fence at the back of the school and then over the ditch at the bottom of Miss Jefferson's wild-flower meadow. Once into the bracken beyond, they were on the track that would take them around the bottom of the Big Hill towards Mister Barney's shack. Jessie led the way, fending off Jack's questions with the same grim determination that drove her tottering legs. She would need all the energy she could muster, all the breath in her body. She could spare none for talking. All the while they could hear the rumble of the convoy as it wound its way out of sight, up the hill past the abbey ruins. Jessie could see them in her mind's eye coming up the road past the end of the farm lane. Panda would be going berserk. She smiled as she thought of him trying to sink his teeth into one of those gigantic digger tyres.

'Jess, what's happening?' Jack was asking again, for the umpteenth time. 'Where are we going?' But she hardly heard him. Her eyes were focused on the ground at her feet. She had to be sure she did not trip. Her heart and her mind were fixed on her plan. It might take fifty days. Fifty days, she'd heard somewhere, was about as long as you could go without food. You had to have water, but there was lots of water where she was going.

Without warning, her knees buckled and then she was struggling to get up. Jack was there, arms under her shoulders, helping her to her feet, then holding her steady. Cross with herself, she shook herself free of him and staggered on. Brambles tugged at her coat, tore at her neck. She bobbed and weaved, trying to dodge them and duck them. She coughed out a fly that she had swallowed and battled on.

It seemed an eternity before they emerged from the track to find themselves in the middle of the grassy clearing, the place where the tracks met. There was the main track up the Big Hill, winding its way through rocks and bracken to the top; and there, just across the clearing from them, stood Mister Barney's shack, the smoke rising from the chimney. They could see the yellow convoy quite clearly now. It had stopped down by the road at the bottom of the hill. And beyond the yellow convoy, nose to tail behind them, were the islanders in their Land-Rovers and pick-ups. And there were people on bikes, and on foot too, dozens of them, all hurrying along the high road and the coast road. The whole island was converging on the Earthbusters.

It was some distance away, but Jessie could see her mother. She was standing in front of the leading digger, talking to the driver. And then she was pushing at it, kicking at it, drumming her fists on it. Jessie's father put his arms round her from behind and turned her towards him. The diggers towered above them, snorting black smoke from their chimneys. Her mother had stopped struggling now, and her father was stroking her hair, then leading her away, her head on his shoulder.

'That's your mom down there, isn't it?' said Jack. Jessie didn't reply. There wasn't the time. The diggers were on the move again.

Jessie couldn't run properly. She'd never been able to run, not like the other children could, but she was as near to it then, going across the clearing, as she'd ever been. She was going so fast now. She couldn't understand why she wasn't falling over, but somehow she wasn't. Somehow her body kept up with her legs and she didn't topple. Jack was having to run to keep up with her. She had worked out the exact spot to do it: where the main track up the Big Hill left the clearing. There were granite posts on either side, and boulders all around – it would be the perfect place. They would *have* to stop. They would have no choice. The diggers were still crawling up the hill. Jessie felt a great surge of joy as she knew for sure that she was going to make it to the clearing before them. There would be time enough too to catch her breath and tell Jack everything she had in mind, her whole plan. Nothing could stop her now. Nothing.

The driver in the first digger was the same driver who had talked to Jack down on the quay a few days before. He was still shaken by what had just happened down by the road. Until recently he had never given a lot of thought as to what his Earthbuster did. He had operated diggers all over Ireland and in England, motorway work mostly, and quarry work sometimes. He loved the power of them, the smell of them. There had been some talk back in Mrs O'Leary's pub where he was staying about the few cranks on the island who didn't want the gold mine. He'd laughed it off like all the other drivers; but after the machines had been tampered with that night, they had all taken it a lot more seriously. He was genuinely puzzled that someone out there hated his machine that much.

And then, just a few moments ago, there was this woman, eyes blazing at him, screaming at him to go back, that what he was doing was an obscenity, a sacrilege. She'd stood there, pushing at his digger, kicking it. He hadn't known what to do, what to say. She'd looked up at him one last time and begged him. 'Please don't do it. Please . . .' He'd revved up his engine so he didn't have to hear any more. He was still thinking about her, wondering what was so special about the hill up ahead that she wanted to save it. He peered up at it. It looked ordinary enough to him, just rocks and gorse and bracken. What was she making such a fuss about?

The boy came out of nowhere, and was waving him down. He braked hard, as hard as he could, and slithered to a stop. He hadn't noticed the girl until then. She was sitting right in the centre of the track over on the far side of the clearing, legs crossed, hands on her knees and still as a statue. The boy was shouting up at him now, and that was when he recognised him. It was the same American lad he had shown over his engine down by the quay. He remembered he had been impressed by how much he knew about engines for a boy of his age.

He turned off the ignition and opened the door of his

cab to give him a piece of his mind, but the boy didn't let him get a word in. 'She says you've got to stop right there, sir. She says you can't go any further.'

The digger driver was suddenly aware of an old man emerging from the door of a shack on the edge of the clearing. He was inching his way down the garden path, balanced between two sticks. If the old man hadn't been there, the digger driver might really have let rip, language and all. He tried to calm himself. 'Will you tell the young lady to shift herself?' he said. 'We've got a job of work to do. We're days late as it is. You tell her, will you?'

'Won't do you much good,' Jack replied. 'See, she doesn't want you here. She doesn't want you digging up the Big Hill. Nothing will change her mind, not when it's made up. And it's made up.' The digger driver felt his anger boiling, but he held on to himself. The old man from the shack was leaning on his gate now, chickens pecking around his boots.

Neither of the children moved a muscle. 'Listen, son,' the digger driver thumbed over his shoulder as he spoke, 'there's three more of these behind. And we've got security men too, a dozen of them. After what's happened, the company's taking no chances. We don't want anyone getting hurt, do we now?' But he could see from their set jaws, their cold, defiant eyes that he was getting nowhere at all. He tried again, a gentler tack. 'Look, all this. It won't do any good, you know.'

Jack interrupted. 'She's not going to let you dig. Isn't that right, Jess? Tell the guy.'

'I'm not going to let you dig,' said Jessie.

'What did I tell you?' said Jack.

By now all the other Earthbusters and Land-Rovers and pick-ups had come to a standstill in a long line that stretched all the way back down the track to the road. Everyone was getting out to find out what was going on, what was holding everything up. They were swarming up the track past the machines and into the clearing. Father Gerald tiptoed round a puddle, his cassock tucked up under his belt. Behind him came Mrs Burke, teetering along in her tight skirt. Liam was there, and Marion Murphy too. They were all there now, every child in the school. They stood and stared, just like everyone else.

Jessie was looking for her mother and father, but she still couldn't see them. She noticed Michael Murphy talking animatedly to one of the digger drivers, and Miss Jefferson was picking up one of the infants – Jessie couldn't see which – who had fallen over and hurt his knee. Very soon the entire clearing was filled with islanders, and digger drivers in their orange overalls, and security men in their blue uniforms and shiny peaked caps – like the Garda, but they weren't. Last of all came Jessie's mother and father, pushing their way through the crowd to the front.

When she saw Jessie sitting there on the path in front of the diggers, she made to rush forward, but Jessie's father held her back. 'No, Cath,' he said. 'She won't come to any harm. I won't let her. But leave her be, eh? Let her do what she has to do.'

Jessie stood up – and that took some time. She had to turn herself on to her stomach and push herself up, first on to her knees and then on to unsteady legs. Jack did not help her. He knew by now that she only liked to be helped in private. As Jessie looked at the expectant crowd in front of her, she felt sick to her stomach and all her courage seemed suddenly to drain from her. Jack smiled his encouragement, but he could see from her eyes that she just could not do it. He knew then he would have to do the talking. There was no other way.

He took a deep breath. 'I guess you're all wondering what Jess and me are doing,' he began. 'Well, we're going to the top of the Big Hill, and we're going to stay up there for just as long as it takes, until the diggers go away. Jess and me, we've both been up there before.' He looked long and hard at Mrs Burke and smiled. 'I stood on top of that hill and I looked around me. Up there it's like you belong, like you're part of something that's been going on for thousands of years. It's special, real special, a living, breathing thing. You cut the top off the Big Hill and you'd be killing it for sure. You dig out the gold, you'd be tearing out its heart. But I guess you know that already.'

The sea sighed and the wind whispered, and the crowd stood stunned and silent. Jack went on. 'I've been thinking a whole lot just lately. My dad's sick, real sick. I've been thinking that maybe he won't make it, and he won't be around any more. And then I started thinking that that's what's going to happen to me too, to Jess, to all of us. It's like we're just passing through, but this hill is here for ever. And we've got to leave it just like we found it. We've got to leave good air to breathe, we've got to leave the fish in the sea, or else there'll soon be nothing left. I'm not making much sense, I guess, but you know what I mean.'

Jack took Jessie's hand in his. 'So Jess, she decided we're going right up to the top of the Big Hill, and once we're up there, we're not moving, no way. If they want that gold, then they'll have to go right over us to get it.' He caught Marion's eye, and smiled at her. 'You can come with us too if you want. You all can. We'd sure like that.' He turned to Jessie. 'Coming?' And they walked away together up the track.

The crowd looked on. No one moved. No one said a

word. A few paces up the track and Jessie felt weak all over. 'Jack,' she whispered. 'I'm trembling.'

'Me too,' said Jack. 'You've thought about this, haven't you? It's a long way to the top, you know.'

'I remember,' said Jessie. Suddenly she gripped his arm. 'Can you feel them, Jack?'

What?

'The ghosts, the pirates. They're here, they're all around us. And she's here too, Grania O'Malley. I can feel her. She's watching, I know she is!' Jack looked around him and then over his shoulder. He stopped. Jessie turned and saw what Jack had already seen. Old Mister Barney was following them up the hill, his white head bent between his sticks. He moved like a tortoise, every ponderous step a massive effort. He paused for a moment and lifted his head to look up at them.

'You mind if I come along?' he said.

Then Jessie's mother was breaking away from the crowd and running up to him. 'I'm coming too,' she said.

Mister Barney smiled at her. 'Just so long as you can keep up with me, Cath,' he said. He waved a stick at Jessie and Jack. 'Don't just stand there. We'll meet you at the top.'

Jessie was looking for her father and could not see him. 'Is Dad coming?' she called out.

'Later,' said her mother. 'He's gone back to fetch some food and drink.'

'Plenty of water up there,' said Jessie, and she turned, balanced herself against Jack and started to climb again.

They were only about halfway up the hill, just past the waterfall, when Jessie felt her legs giving out on her. She was leaning more and more on Jack now, and stopping every few steps. 'I don't think I'm going to make it,' she breathed.

'You've got to,' said Jack, his arm tightening round her. 'She's watching, remember? Everyone's watching.' That was when she turned to look. Jack was wrong. True, some of them were still standing by the diggers and watching, but most of those wore the orange of the drivers or the blue of the security guards. Michael Murphy was with them, and a few other islanders – but only a few. Jessie was wondering where the rest had gone, when she saw them, dozens of them, coming around the bend in the track. Liam was running on ahead, waving to them. Father Gerald was alongside old Mister Barney now, with Jessie's mother. And Mrs Burke was just behind them, her skirt hitched up, Miss Jefferson striding past her. 'Will you look at that?' Jessie breathed. 'They're coming, they're coming with us.'

'So?' said Jack. 'What are you waiting for? Do you

want Marion Murphy to beat you to the top?'

'She's not there, is she?'

'I don't know, but she could be.' That was enough of a spur for Jessie. She lurched on, calling out the rhythm as she went: 'One and two. One and two. One and two.' She scrambled on hands and knees over the rocky places, and then dragged herself to her feet, hauling on anything Jack offered her – an arm, a leg, trousers, anything. On she staggered with never a look behind her now. She could hear them coming. She didn't need to look.

In the end she wasn't first to the top. She had the first sight of it, and felt that warm tingle of exhilaration, of triumph, when Panda came bounding past her, knocking into her and sending her crumpling to the ground. She bellowed at him, but he never even stopped to look at her. Mole was trotting up the track towards them, his great ears pricked. When he saw Panda ahead of him, he raced on past them, head lowered, ears back, chasing him round and round the top of the Big Hill, Panda dancing away from him and barking wildly.

By the time Jessie and Jack got there themselves, Panda was lying down, panting and happy on the thrift, and Mole was browsing busily in the undergrowth near by, his tail whisking at the flies. Jack had a drink from the spring above the rock pool. He sat back on his haunches, wiping his mouth with the back of his hand.

'No earrings this time,' he said. Jessie was stretched out on her back still fighting for her breath.

'I can hear them,' said Jack getting to his feet. 'They're coming.' But Jessie could hear someone else, someone much closer. She propped herself up on to her elbows.

'Listen Jack,' she whispered. 'Listen.'

The voice was right beside them. 'Jessie? Jack? You've done fine, just fine.' It was *her*. It was *her*. The voice went on. 'We're all mighty pleased with you. But now you've got the high ground, you have to hold on to it, d'you hear me? Believe me, I know. Once you got the high ground, you don't give it up, no matter what. And don't let them talk you down. They'll try it for sure.'

'We won't,' said Jessie, looking around her, hoping she would appear. 'We promise we won't.' There was no sign of her, so Jessie went on, 'It *was* you that dug up the treasure, wasn't it?'

The voice laughed. 'Well, as you know, the boys weren't at all pleased about the idea of parting with it in the first place. They were happy enough to dig it up. Lots of "I told you sos," but there we are, that's the luck of the game. I thought myself it was a fine idea, and it would have been too. All those rules and regulations. A lot of rot. Ah well, it was a nice try; but this is better, much

180

better, and this'll work. So you just sit tight now, y'hear me?'

'Can't we see you?' It wasn't at all comfortable, talking to a voice.

'Soon enough, you'll see me soon enough, when you need to. I'll be seeing you.'

'Grania O'Malley! Grania O'Malley!' But there was no reply. Jessie turned to Jack. 'You heard her, Jack? You did hear her?' Jack was nodding, his eyes darting nervously.

'I wish she wouldn't go all invisible on us,' he said. 'It scares the hell out of me when she does that.' She took his hand and gripped it. She squeezed twice and he did the same. They were together in this, in this as in everything. Both of them felt it at the same moment.

And that was how Father Gerald found the two children some moments later, sitting exhausted but exhilarated, hand in hand beside the rock pool.

'You won't talk us down, Father,' said Jessie, as he came towards her.

'I wouldn't want to, Jessie, even if I could,' he said, his sermon smile on his face, a smile Jessie had never believed was real, until now. 'There's half the island coming up the track. I don't know about them, but I've come to stay, and I'm staying put till the diggers go.'

'Where's Mum?' Jessie asked.

'She's way back down the hill with Mister Barney. Someone went back for his wheelbarrow – he just couldn't go any further, not under his own steam. He didn't like the idea of the wheelbarrow that much, not at first. "Jessie goes by wheelbarrow sometimes," says your mother. And he says: "Well then, if it's good enough for her, it's good enough for me." They won't be long. What you said about your father back there, Jack . . . Opened our eyes, so you did. You made us all do some thinking.'

Very soon the top of the Big Hill was crowded with people, all milling about in excited huddles. More would be coming, they said. Like Jessie's father, many had gone back for tents and blankets and food. Someone started clapping and then everyone was cheering. That was when Jessie saw her mother pushing the wheelbarrow up over the top of the hill towards her, Mister Barney waving like an emperor. They helped him out, and gave him his sticks.

'Well,' said Mister Barney looking around him, 'it's the first time I've been up here in over twenty years. And if they want to get me down again, then they'll just have to drag me.' He nodded towards Jessie and Jack and smiled, his eyes full of tears as he spoke. 'If I had my hat, then I'd take it off to the two of you. And I've not taken my hat off to anyone in all my life.'

Jessie felt Jack's hand-squeeze and responded in kind without looking at him. She was tired. The muscles in her legs were cold now and cramping, but she had never felt so happy. Mister Barney had just finished speaking, and the clapping had scarcely died away, when they were aware of a dozen men standing at the top of the track, most of them in blue uniforms and shiny peaked caps.

'All right.' It was Michael Murphy, beside himself with fury. 'I've had enough. First of all you sabotaged the diggers, and now this. This is my hill you're on, and I've a legal right to do with it what I will. I've had enough of it, do you hear me?' He paused, and then added heavily, threateningly, 'You stay up here, and things could turn nasty. People could get hurt. Do you understand my drift?' He seemed to calm down a little. 'Listen, I'll let you stay here the night so's you can make your point, but I want you off this hill by the morning, you hear me now?'

For some time no one responded, everyone looking to everyone else. Then Jessie's mother walked right up to him.

'You're not welcome here, Michael Murphy,' she said. 'This may be *your* hill, but this is *our* island, and we all say we're not moving from here until your diggers leave. Now is that clear enough?'

It must have been, because Michael Murphy turned on his heel and walked away down the track, taking the men in blue with him, Panda yapping at their heels.

'I'm cold,' said Jessie, drawing her knees up to her chest and clasping them to her.

'You want me to rub your legs?' Jack asked. 'They hurting?'

But Jessie didn't get a chance to reply. Someone was standing in front of them, in a pair of pale green trainers. She looked up. It was Marion Murphy, and she'd been crying. 'I came, Jack,' she said. 'After what you said, I came. And I'm going to tell my dad to put a stop to it. I'll be back later. I'll bring back some chocolate, shall I? I've got a duvet at home, Jessie, if you want.'

'That would be great,' said Jessie, and she smiled at Marion Murphy for the first time in her whole life.

11 THE BATTLE OF THE EARTHBUSTERS

BY THE TIME DARKNESS FELL THAT NIGHT, THE top of the Big Hill had become a village of tents and makeshift huts. It was a fine, dry night, but there was a cold breeze off the sea and they were soon glad of all the cover they had built, and of the fire too. Father Gerald had appointed himself keeper of the fire, and sent every child he could recruit scavenging all over the hill. But the brushwood they found was too small and too dry, and burnt too quickly. There just wasn't enough of it to keep the fire going. So Jessie's father, who had already made several supply trips up and down the hill with the tractor and link box, went off back down the hill again to load up with peat.

Jessie sat in the mouth of her hut next to Jack, both of them swathed in blankets. The hut was built into the rocks, with a bracken roof and a bracken floor. She breathed in deep the warmth of the fire, and at last began to feel her feet again. She was watching the shadows round the fire, hoping always that one of them might materialise sooner or later into Grania O'Malley. But the shadows remained shadows and she didn't come. Mrs O'Leary had brought her barbeque up from the pub and was grilling hundreds of sausages over a bank of glowing coals, with Panda sitting, ears pricked and expectant, right beside her.

'Do you want one?' said Jack.

'Two,' replied Jessie, 'and that's just for starters.' And he left her there alone, gazing deep into the fire. She was conscious of the tractor coming back up the hill, its lights sweeping the bracken, and then her father's voice calling for help to unload. Mrs O'Leary was bellowing that the sausages were well done, that there were beans and bread to go with them, that everyone should come and get it. Shadows flitted past the fire towards the barbeque. 'And Mrs Burke's doing the drinks, by the rock pool,' Mrs O'Leary announced. 'And there's potatoes baking in the fire.'

'Quite a party,' said a voice. There was no one there,

not at first; but then Grania O'Malley was suddenly sitting right beside Jessie, holding her hands out towards the fire and rubbing them together. 'That's a proper fire too.'

'They'll see you!' said Jessie.

'What if they do? And anyway who's looking? They're all after the sausages. And besides, to see me, you've got to want to see me; and what's more I've got to want you to see me. When they want to see me, and I want them to see me, then they'll see me, but only then – if you see what I'm saying?' Jessie certainly did not, but she wasn't going to say so. 'Listen, Jess,' she went on, 'I may not have time for this tomorrow. I want you to have this.' And she took Jessie's hand and pressed something into it, something hard and cold and sharp.

'What is it?'

'An arrowhead. No it's not Jack's. The boys and me, we looked for it everywhere. Couldn't find it. But maybe this one'll be just as lucky for him. You tell him what you like. You're good enough at the tale-telling – I've heard you. He won't know the difference.'

'Where did you get it?'

'America, just like he did. From the arrow the Indians shot at me. Missed me by a whisker, like I told you; but I kept it. My lucky charm, you might say. It worked a treat for me all my life, maybe it will for Jack.' She closed Jessie's fingers round it and smiled into the fire. 'The night before the battle, just like the old days. The times I've sat up here waiting for the enemy, and we always saw them off, always. I'll be with you in spirit tomorrow, Jess, you can be sure of that.'

'But there won't be a real battle, will there? No one'll really get hurt, will they?' Jessie asked. But when she looked, there was no one there to answer her.

Her father was walking towards her, dusting his hands off on his trousers. 'Strange,' he said. 'I was just unloading the peat a few moments ago, and suddenly there was this woman helping me – long hair, cloak round her shoulders. Don't know who she was. Never seen her before in my life. She said something though, like she knew me, like she knew you. She said I was a very lucky man to have a daughter like you. You know who she is? You seen her?' Jessie shook her head. Her father went on. 'A vision, I expect. She's right though, I am a lucky man. You're the daughter of your mother, I'd say.'

'And who else should she be the daughter of?' Jessie's mother said, coming out of the dark into the light of the fire. Jack was with her, and he was carrying a plate piled high with sausages and beans.

They called old Mister Barney over to join them, and he sat with them round the communal plate and dug in just like they did, fingers for the sausages and the one spoon to share for the baked beans. Jack pigged himself on the sausages. There wasn't a mention, Jessie noticed, of peanut butter sandwiches. When she pointed this out, Jack smiled wryly and said in his best Irish: 'Bog off, why don't you!' They were still laughing when Liam came round with potatoes. They were supposed to be baked, but they were more burnt than baked. They ate them all the same.

'Like the feeding of the five thousand,' said Father Gerald as he passed by. He wasn't far wrong too. The food seemed to have arrived miraculously, enough for everyone; and, from the spring above the rock pool, all the water they needed to wash it down. Mister Barney burped, apologised, and drank some more water.

'That's the best water in all the world, make no mistake,' he said. 'If I live to be a hundred, and it's not far off now, it'll be because of that water. Life-giving, that's what it is. They get digging with their infernal machines, and they'll poison it for ever. Have some, Jessie, have some while you can.' And he passed on the mug to Jessie. Jessie had never thought much about water before. Water had always been just water. It came out of the sky, and there was always plenty of it. She'd drunk it often enough, but now she was tasting it for the first time. It wasn't bitter like other drinks, it wasn't sweet like other drinks. It was cold and it was clean. Whether it was the water or not, Jessie did not know; but she felt a sudden and over-powering sense of complete well-being.

The sausage and bean feast went on well into the night. No one talked of what might happen the next day. With everyone in such high spirits round the fire, Jessie thought she must be the only one even thinking of tomorrow. She could see Jack fooling around in the darkness beyond the great fire with Liam and all the others. She wanted to get him on his own, to give him Grania O'Malley's lucky arrowhead, and to warn him about the battle. When the sausages and beans were exhausted at last, Miss Jefferson got out her squeezebox, and they sang all the songs they knew, and a few they didn't as well. Then there was the dancing, everyone clapping out the rhythm as the feet flashed and flickered in the firelight. In the dying of the fire it warmed their hearts, and their bodies too.

But it was a different matter when it was over. They crawled into their tents and their huts, and wrapped themselves up in their blankets against the cold and the damp. Once the urgent whisperings and the suppressed giggles stopped – and it wasn't long – then the night was filled with a heavy, ominous silence. Jessie snuggled up to her mother on the bracken. Her father and Mister Barney were lying head to toe beside them; and Jack was stretched out at her feet, head in the crook of his arm and facing away from her. He was asleep already, but she didn't want him to be. She kept prodding his side with her toe. She had to find some way to talk to him, she had to. Then she heard him snoring, and knew there was no point any more. She would tell him everything in the morning. Her last prayer that night was to Grania O'Malley, that if there had to be a battle, then please, she didn't want anyone to get hurt.

She was woken suddenly. Someone was calling her name. Marion Murphy was inside the hut and bending over her, tear-stained and crying.

'What is it, Marion?' said Jessie's mother, sitting up.

Marion was looking at Jessie. 'I couldn't come last night. I tried, Jessie, honest.' She was breathless with crying. 'My dad, he caught me with the duvet. He locked me in my room. I wanted to come.'

'It's all right, Marion,' said Jessie's mother.

'No.' Marion was shaking her head vigorously. 'It's not, it's not. You don't understand. They're coming.

They've got over more of those men, those security men. They came last night on the ferry. There's a whole army of them now, and they're coming for you. I heard them plan it, the Earthbusters first, like tanks, and everyone else behind. They're coming, they're coming now. They want to surprise you. I jumped out of my window. I hurt my arm.' Jessie's father was already pulling on his boots and crawling out of the hut. He patted Marion's head as he passed.

'Good girl,' he said. 'Good girl.'

Jessie smiled at Marion. 'You staying then, are you?' she said.

'If you want me?' Marion was looking at Jack.

'Course we do, don't we, Jack?' said Jessie. 'If there's going to be a battle, then we'll need all the good fighters we can get.'

'Who said anything about a fight?' Jessie's mother spoke sharply. 'This thing's got to be settled peacefully. I don't want anyone else getting hurt. Now let's have a look at that arm, Marion.'

There were no sausages left for breakfast, and no beans – they'd eaten them all. So everyone chewed on a cold charred potato or two, then cupped their hands under the spring, and had a long, cool drink of water to wash away the taste. Where the baseball bat appeared from, no one knew; but Liam was brandishing it around his head. And that wasn't the only weapon Jessie had noticed. There were garden forks, iron pokers and several long sticks sharpened into lances. They watched and they waited. There was, in the cold light of that dawn, a sense of awful expectation. When they heard the engines starting up at the bottom of the Big Hill, they gathered together, as sheep do, for protection. Jessie was frightened, frightened by what she had started, by what might happen. There was no stopping it now.

Her mother spoke out, her voice ringing with authority. 'We'll drop the weapons, all of them. We'll not be needing them. There'll be none of that.' Liam took some time to drop the baseball bat. When at last he did, then all the others, grown-ups and children, followed suit. 'We'll join hands, shall we?' said Jessie's mother. 'We'll make a circle, a circle round the top of the Big Hill that no one can break.' Jessie found Jack beside her and took his hand. She had her father on the other side. She clung to both of them, and just hoped. Only Mister Barney did not join in the circle. Leaning on his sticks, he stood in the middle like some ancient chieftain, Jessie thought. They could see the first puffs of black smoke now above the bracken and glimpses of yellow as the Earthbusters came grinding on slowly, inexorably, up the hill towards them.

Some, like Father Gerald, closed their eyes and prayed, while the gulls wheeled overhead, screaming, echoing the fear in their hearts. Then a voice came from behind them, clear and firm. It was Mister Barney. 'We'll see them off. We'll see them off, so we will. Stand firm, hold the line, and we'll send them packing.'

And then they saw the first Earthbuster rearing up the track towards them. Panda barked at it furiously, hackles raised. There was an initial, instinctive step backwards, but that only served to close the circle and tighten it. With arms linked now, they watched the first digger move on to the top of the Big Hill, crushing the bracken, bumping over the rocks towards them. It wasn't long before they found themselves completely surrounded. Michael Murphy was there, flanked by hard-faced security guards, a small army of them, just as Marion had said. The engines died and a stillness fell over the hill. Even the gulls were silent.

Michael Murphy was flushed in the face even more than usual, and it was the flush of rage. 'What the devil's the matter with you people?' he began. 'You all agreed, didn't you? Well, almost all of you anyway? How come you changed your mind, eh? Just because of what Jack said? He doesn't even live here. Haven't I told you and told you? This gold mine will bring us all work, keep the island going, just like the salmon farm did.' No one spoke. They only stared. Michael Murphy felt the resentment in their eyes, and their fierce determination. There was desperation in his voice now. 'For God's sake, didn't I say we'd put it right after? You won't even notice the difference, I promise you. The Big Hill will be here, just the same, and everyone will have their share of the gold, just like I promised. What more do you want?'

Then Mister Barney spoke up: 'But aren't I right in thinking that you'll be getting a bigger share than anyone else, Mr Murphy?'

Michael Murphy was blazing now. 'It's my hill, isn't it? I own it, don't I? And it's my money brought these diggers here, so it's my risk. Yes, so I'll do well out of it, but so will everyone, we all will. But I'll not stand here bandying words with a mad old fool like you. Now, are you moving or not?'

'Not,' said Jessie's mother firmly. 'What are you going to do, Michael? Set your men on us? You always were a bit of a bully, you know that?'

Suddenly Marion broke the circle and ran crying towards her father. 'Dad, please, please.' She was pleading with him, tugging on his arm, but he wouldn't even look at her. He waved a command to the Earthbusters. The engines fired up again, exhausts belching, then great

195

yellow arms unfolding and stretching out, scoops lowered and poised for digging.

High in the cab, the driver of the first Earthbuster recognised the lady in front of him. She was the same one who had screamed at him and kicked at his digger. The boy was there too, the American boy, and the girl with the limp beside him, arms linked. He lowered his scoop to the ground like the others, an eye on Mr Murphy, watching for the signal to stop. The plan had been clear. They would dig round them, and then move in slowly, scraping away the earth at their feet, just close enough to scare them. But it wasn't working. Frightened or not, they weren't moving. None of them were. Some of the children were crying, mothers and fathers holding them now, trying to comfort them. The digger driver thought of his children back home in Dublin, and he did not like what he was doing. He wouldn't do it. He wouldn't go on.

He was reaching for the ignition key when he saw them out of the corner of his eye. From out of nowhere they seemed to come: twenty, thirty men maybe. Swords drawn, they were striding through the circle, but somehow without breaking it. Then some of them were heading straight towards him. The digger driver knew them at once for what they must be, even though it was impossible in this day and age, quite impossible. Pirates, pirates straight out of the books he read his children. Baggy breeches, barefoot, some of them bearded, and even one with a black eyepatch. They were charging now, swords slicing the air, and yelling a bloodcurdling war-cry that sent warm shivers of fear up his back. The digger driver could not move. He wanted to run, but terror had frozen him to his seat. He looked towards Michael Murphy for help; but Michael Murphy was standing there, aghast, the blood drained from his face.

There was a flag fluttering from the centre of the circle now, a black flag with a red pig on it; and beside the flag stood a tall figure of a woman with a mass of black hair, and there was a sword in her hand too. The pirates were all around his digger now. They were climbing up on to it. One of them had his hand on the cab door, and wrenched it open.

'Nice morning,' said the pirate. 'I wonder if you'd care to step down for a little while?' There was an unpleasant smile on his face. He had very few teeth, and those he did have were like yellow claws. 'Out,' he said. The digger driver did not hesitate, and neither did any of the others. Every digger was soon occupied by pirates, who clambered all over them, waving their swords in wild abandon and whooping in triumph. Michael Murphy and his uniformed army were entirely surrounded by pirates, who tickled them with the points of their swords, under their arms, under their chins, teasing them with terror.

That was when the woman by the flag spoke up. 'Easy boys, easy boys, easy . . . We wouldn't want to frighten them, would we? Well, maybe just a little we would, but not so it hurts, eh?' She turned to Mister Barney. 'Hello, Mister Barney. And how are you this fine morning?' Mister Barney tried to say something. His mouth moved but no sound came out. 'Mister Barney knows well enough who I am – we've met before – and so do Jess and Jack.' She smiled at Jessie.

'By the look on your faces, there's some of you maybe wondering who we are. Well, I'll tell you. My name is Grania O'Malley. And these are my men, my boys. This is our island. This is our hill you're standing on, mine and my forebears', mine and my descendants'. And you,' she went on, sweeping her sword all around her, 'you are my descendants. You are too, Michael Murphy, and you should be ashamed of yourself.' She was pointing her sword straight at him. 'No one owns land, Michael Murphy. You look after it, you protect it for those who come after you, that's all. Can you not understand that?

That is why I'll not let you cut off the head of this hill, why I won't let you tear the heart out of it, not for a pot of gold, not for anything.' Jessie wanted to run to her and hug her, out of sheer relief, out of pure love.

'Now, as I see it, Michael Murphy,' Grania O'Malley went on, 'the good people of Clare have given this a lot of thought. Maybe some of them have come to their senses more slowly than others, but no matter. They have decided they want you to leave and take your machines with you, that they want to keep the Big Hill as it is. They asked you nicely – I heard them. But you didn't listen. If you had listened, then there'd have been no need for me to go sticking my piratical nose in, would there now? As it is, I'm going to have to give a little helping hand.' And, with a wink at Jessie, she said, 'You'll enjoy this, I think, Jess.' Then she whipped up her sword and flashed it above her head. 'Right, boys. You know what to do. But take care now.'

All the engines started up at once. Every digger had a crew of pirates, one in the cab and others sitting on the sides, legs dangling. Grania O'Malley took up her flag and strode forward. 'They've been dying to do this ever since they saw those machines. Little boys at heart, just little boys.'

The Earthbusters were on the move, manoeuvring so

that they were soon lined up and facing towards the cliff-tops, the pirates hanging on to anything they could. The engines revved to full, thunderous throttle; and then, as if unleashed, they lurched forward into the bracken, bumping over the rocks, in a helter-skelter race for the cliffs. The pirates leapt off this way and that, diving off the sides and out of the cabs, into the bracken and rolling away. Everyone was rushing to look. Jessie was just in time to see the first of the Earthbusters flying out over the cliff and somersaulting through the air. The others were soon to follow. Jack was hoping there would be massive explosions, but there weren't. Instead, there were four spectacular splashes, and a lot of steaming and hissing, as the diggers sank slowly into the sea and disappeared.

It was a moment or two before they all realised what had happened, before the cheering began. When it did, it was deafening. Everyone jumped up and down and hugged each other, everyone that is except Michael Murphy and his blue and orange army. Jessie felt herself swept off her feet, and then she was swinging in the air, round and round and round until she was giddy with it and begged to be let down. Grania O'Malley set her on her feet and held her fast by the shoulders so she didn't tumble over.

'I think,' said Grania O'Malley, 'I think the enemy has decided they've had enough. Take a look.' And sure enough, there wasn't a sign either of Michael Murphy, nor of his blue-uniformed security guards, nor of the orange-overalled drivers. The battle was over, over before it had begun.

One by one the pirates gathered around Grania O'Malley from all over the Big Hill. One of them said he had never had so much fun in all his life – nor since, he added with a laugh. Grania O'Malley was talking to Jessie's mother and Mister Barney. Everyone else, Jessie noticed, was keeping their distance from her. They stood together in hushed and huddled groups, eyes wide with wonder and fear.

'Well, you'll not be needing us any more, will you?' Grania O'Malley was saying. 'I think we'd better be going. No sensible ghost wants to outstay her welcome. Now where's that daughter of yours, and where's Jack?' She turned, saw them and held out her arms. Like it or not, and he wasn't at all sure he did, Jack was clasped in an enveloping hug. 'Give my best to America when you see it, Jack,' she said, and she released him. 'Maybe I'll pay you a visit one day. How would that be?'

'Great,' said Jack. 'I know a lot of people who'd like to meet you.'

'We'll see, we'll see,' said Grania O'Malley. And she smiled sadly down at Jessie. 'All good things have to come to an end, Jessie. Look after the place for me, won't you?' She bent down, put her arms round Jessie and held her close. Jessie clung to her. 'I'll be seeing you,' Grania O'Malley whispered. And then, quite suddenly, there was nothing to cling to any more. Jessie looked around her. Grania O'Malley was gone, and her pirates with her.

Everyone thought they had gone for good. They were still standing, stunned by all they had seen, by all that had happened, when Marion grasped Jessie by the arm and pointed out to sea. The galley, under full sail, was moving out over the mist-covered sea towards Clew Bay, towards Rockfleet in the distance, the oars dipping together. Grania O'Malley was standing in the prow of the galley, her flag fluttering above her, her hand raised in farewell. The galley sailed on, drawn slowly into the mist, until they saw it no more.

Jessie felt Jack beside her. 'We won't see her again, will we?' she said.

'Never can tell, not with her,' Jack replied.

'She wanted me to give you this,' said Jessie, taking his hand and laying the arrowhead on his open palm.

'Where? Where did she find it?'

Jessie shrugged her shoulders. 'She didn't say.' She

thought it safer to change the subject before he could ask any more about it. 'We've done it, haven't we?' She looked up at him and smiled. 'We've saved the Big Hill.' But Jack turned away and looked out to the open sea.

'I don't want to go home,' he said. 'I don't ever want to go home.'

'You haven't got to, not yet,' Jessie replied. 'You've got three weeks still.'

Mrs Burke was standing there, barefoot, her shoes dangling from her fingers. 'Well, Jessie Parsons,' she said. 'You *can* climb the Big Hill, and I'm going to have to eat a lot of humble pie, aren't I? I'm going to write you a hundred lines, Jessie, and do you know what they'll say? "There's more things in heaven and earth than are dreamt of in your philosophy, Mrs Burke." That's Shakespeare, you know,' she added with a smile. And Jessie remembered then that Grania O'Malley had once quoted Shakespeare to her, and tried to remember what it was. Then it came to her, and she said it out loud.

' "Parting is such sweet sorrow," that's Shakespeare.'

'So it is,' said Mrs Burke, wide-eyed with amazement, 'so it is.'

Mrs Burke was a changed woman after the 'Battle of the Earthbusters', as it came to be called. She ended term a day early – 'by decree,' she said, 'by Burke's decree' – and of course no one argued. So Jack had almost three weeks of baseball and rollerblading and fixing Clatterbang. He was happiest chatting away to Jessie, with his hands deep inside Clatterbang's clapped-out engine, trying to repair the unrepairable.

Marion came over often now. It was very strange, Jessie thought, how fascinated Marion Murphy had suddenly become by carburettors and exhaust systems and brake pads, very strange indeed! Jessie didn't mind so much now. She couldn't bring herself to like Marion, but at least she had stopped fearing her. Much as they might have liked to, neither Marion nor Jessie could keep Jack entirely for themselves. Everyone else wanted him on the baseball field, particularly now that the gloves, and the New York Yankee caps had arrived from home, along with a real baseball ball.

Of course the newspapers had a field day. Journalists came from all over the world. Clare Island became known as 'Ghost Island'. Everyone had a story to tell. Ghost-hunting tourists came over in their droves and went on treks up the Big Hill. But journalist or tourist, they all went away disappointed, concluding that the islanders were all conspiring together to spin them a fantastic yarn, that there had been no ghost pirates at all, that the islanders had simply dressed up as pirates, terrified the digger drivers and then run the Earthbusters off the cliffs themselves. In time, even some of the islanders themselves began to doubt the evidence of their own memories.

There was a last baseball game on the field – the Pirates (the children, including Jack and Liam and Marion) against the Earthbusters (the grown-ups, including Jessie's father, Father Gerald and Miss Jefferson). The Pirates won, but only because Jack hit four home runs, and pitched with such venom that the Earthbusters barely saw the ball. Pirates 4, Earthbusters 0. As Father Gerald pointed out, exactly the same score as the Battle of the Earthbusters.

After the game, they had an American-style barbeque on the field with fried chicken and beefburgers and Coke – and peanut butter sandwiches. Almost everyone was there, and it didn't rain either. Even Mister Barney came along. They all watched and clapped as he drank down his very first Coke. He said afterwards that it would be his last, quite definitely his last. It was like bog water, he said, with sugar in it; but that all the same, it had given him an idea, a wonderful idea. He would keep the idea to himself, he said, until he had it all worked out.

*   *   *

The next day, Mister Barney was there on the quayside, along with everyone else, to wave Jack off. Jessie had insisted on going with her mother to see Jack on to his plane at Shannon. It was a grey drizzly day, with the waves heaving and the mainland invisible behind the mist. Jack told Liam he had to keep the Pirates going, he had to make them practise, because he would be back. And Jessie knew he wasn't just saying that. For the first time in his life, Liam didn't seem to know what to say. Marion just hugged Jack quickly, and ran off. Jessie's father thanked him for all he had done, and for his work on Clatterbang.

'I won't say it goes a lot better, Jack,' he said. 'You'd need a miracle for that, and I think we've used up all the miracles due to us, don't you? But the exhaust sounds different, I'll give you that. Ruder.'

As the ferry moved out of the harbour and into the swell of the ocean, the goodbyes dying on the wind, Jessie began to wish she had stayed at home. Jack seemed so sunk in himself. He kept turning the arrowhead over and over in his fingers, and hardly looked up at all. Once back on the mainland, they sat side by side in the back of the car. She had so much to say, but could say nothing. They would catch each other's eye from time to time to try to smile, but they couldn't. Jessie was crying inside already.

She just hoped she would be able to manage a smile when the time came to say goodbye.

At the departure gate at Shannon Airport there was a panic about his passport before Jessie's mother found it in a sidepocket of his bag. 'A pity,' she smiled ruefully. 'We could all have gone home again for peanut butter sandwiches and Coke. We're going to miss you so much, Jack. Give my love to your dad, won't you?' And she hugged him tight. 'God bless,' she said.

Jack put his baseball hat on Jessie head, fixed it sideways at the proper angle, and said, 'See you, Jess.' He walked backwards for a few steps. 'I'll write you,' he called out. He waved once and was gone. And she hadn't even said what she had meant to say, that she hoped his father would get better.

He did write, but not for some time. Jessie searched through the post whenever it came, but it was over a month before Jack's letter finally arrived. Jessie ripped it open and read:

> Dear Jess,
> I had a great time. I met just about the best friend I'll ever have too – and I'm not talking about Liam or Marion. They're good guys, but I'm talking about you.

Are you sure what happened up on the Big Hill really did happen? Sometimes, now I'm back home, I think the whole thing was just one wild dream. It wasn't, was it? I'm glad it wasn't only you and me that saw her – her and her pirates. I guess if everyone else saw them, then it really did happen, didn't it?

I've still got the arrowhead, only it isn't mine, is it? I thought it was, but mine had the point chipped off. But I figured it out. It's Grania O'Malley's, isn't it? She gave it to you, and you gave it to me, and you had to pretend it was my lucky arrowhead, the one I lost. Well, if you see her, will you tell her thank you, and tell her that her arrowhead is a lot luckier than mine was. When I had mine, Dad was sick and getting sicker. Now he's a lot better after his surgery, and better every day. He's smiling again. He says the new valve in his heart is real state of the art, and better than anything I've got in my VW Bug. Some arrowhead!

After what happened with you, the treasure and the Big Hill and all, I don't believe things just happen. I think maybe we can help make them happen. Next year I want you to come over to Long Island. I've asked Dad, and he says yes. I'll show you my VW Bug. OK, so I know you're not that interested, but I'm going to show you anyway. We'll go sailing and I'll take you Rollerblading in Central Park. But I can't promise you ghosts.

The other day I told Mrs Cody – she's my teacher, remember? – that during the vacation I found out it was the Irish, an Irish pirate called Grania O'Malley, who discovered America first, and not the Dutch, not the French, not the British. She told me it was all just wishful thinking – the Irish blood in me. She'd never even heard of Grania O'Malley. One day I'm going to prove it, not just to her, but to everyone, then no one will be able to argue.

I hope you're getting along with Marion – she wasn't too bad after all, was she? Say hi to your folks and to Liam and all the guys. And a big hi to you and to Mole and to that stinky old dog of yours.

Love,

Jack.

Jessie sat down and replied at once, on Miss Jefferson's word processor which she had been practising on, and which she now found a lot easier than writing by hand.

Dear Jack,

Thanks for your letter. A lot's happened. You'll never

guess. It's about the Big Hill. It was old Mister Barney's idea. My dad took him (and me) along to see Marion's dad, because he's the only one with the money to set it up, and because Mister Barney says you can't be blaming him for ever, that it was everyone's fault, not just Mr Murphy's. Anyway, we went to see him. He wasn't too happy at first. Then Mister Barney told him his plan, and he got happier by the minute.

Mister Barney said how he'd been thinking about Coke and how horrible it was, but how everyone else in the world seemed to love it. And there was the best and purest water in the world, pouring down the Big Hill and going nowhere in particular. How about we set up a bottling plant, and sell it? We'll call it 'Grania'. We'll have her picture on the label and sell it all over the world. we'll make a whole pile of money for everyone on the island, including Mr Murphy – lots of jobs and all that – and we'll not have to shift a single rock on the Big Hill.

Mr Murphy offered him a whisky and old Mister Barney said he'd rather have water – you live longer, he said. I can't help thinking that Grania must have put the idea into his head. After all, she did just about everything else, didn't she? I'll send you over a bottle of 'Grania' soon as they start bottling it – probably be next spring, Dad says.

We've still got lots of people coming over to Clare looking for ghosts. There were some Americans here last week. They came for tea, so we gave them the last of the peanut butter. They didn't seem to like it much. They asked me lots of questions and they had a recording machine on. Afterwards they told us they were from Los Angeles, and they made films. They said they might make a film all about the ghost of Grania O'Malley and the Big Hill, and if they did they'd film it here on the island. Dad says it's a pipe dream. Grania O'Malley smoked a pipe, didn't she?

Mole and Panda send you lots of love and so do Mum and Dad (and Marion of course) and so do I. And yes, I'd love to come to Long Island as long as I don't have to get oily hands, if you know what I mean. Mum says it's a bit expensive, so maybe I'll come over by boat, by galley, and surprise you. We've got some-one here who's been before remember? So she knows the way. I'll ask her when I next see her, shall I?

See you soon,

Love from Jessie.

PS I haven't seen her again, but she's been here. I was

changing Barry's water last Sunday, and I found my two earrings under the stones. I wear them all the time. Dad says I look a million dollars. And he's right too.

POSTSCRIPT

Grania O'Malley and Clare Island

Of all the characters in this book, the only one who *really* lived was Grania O'Malley herself. She was a pirate queen who, for many years, held sway all along the coast of Mayo and Galway, and in Clew Bay in particular. In her long life – she lived from 1530–1603 – she had many galleys, many castles (amongst them one on Clare Island and one at Rockfleet, both still there), and she had many husbands too. The English called her Grace O'Malley, the Irish Grany O'Malley – pronounced Grania. She *did* have a son called Tibbott and he *was* imprisoned by the English. She *did* go to Greenwich in London to seek his release from Queen Elizabeth. So the two pirate queens met. No one knows what passed between them, only that some months later Tibbott was released.

An Armada galleon *was* wrecked off Clare Island in 1588, and there *was* treasure on board. In April of 1994 I went to Clare Island with my wife. We were not looking for treasure, but to see where Grania O'Malley had lived. We found a kindly people who took us in out of the driving rain, fed us and helped us with our research. Many of them were called O'Malley. We saw the 'Big Hill', as they call it. We went into the ruined abbey. We saw Grania O'Malley's grave. There's a school close by. We visited her castle. We heard there'd been gold found on the nearby island of Inishturk. We found the spirit of Grania O'Malley alive all over the island. That's why I came back home and wrote this story.

None of the Clare Island people in the story are real of course, but the place is; and as for Grania O'Malley, she's as real as you or me; as real as you want her to be.

M.M.
September 1995